THE SLAVE MURNO FINDS IS DEAD. SAV-
AGED BY THE HUNTING BRELOONS, HE
HAD BEEN HUNG UPSIDE DOWN TO DIE.

To Murno it looks like a trap. Have the Gaddyl—the
alien conquerors of Earth—discovered that freedmen
are helping runaway slaves escape? If so, men like Muro
and their families will be shown no mercy.

But Murno learns that the danger is even greater than
he had feared. Unless Omha—the legendary savior of
mankind—can rid the world of the alien oppressors, all
mankind will be exterminated. But who, or what, is
Omha? And how can Murno, on foot and armed only
with primitive weapons, escape the technologically advanced Gaddyl long enough to find and awaken Omha,
the sleeping god?

OMHA ABIDES

by C. C. MaCapp

PAPERBACK LIBRARY, INC.

NEW YORK

CHAPTER I: THE SLAVE ESCAPE

Murno was suddenly awake, in the uneasy hour before dawn, a faint echo of terror in his brain. Quietly, so as not to disturb Klayr and the children, he rolled from his bunk; crept to the window that faced west, and cautiously parted the handmade wooden shutters a crack.

The nearly-full moon, blurred by mist, hung just above the ridge of wooded hills so that this slope was in black shadow. Closer, the lush grass in the narrow valley, still wet with the night's rain, rippled fitfully. He saw no sign of anything threatening in the valley.

Then the sound that had awakened him came again, born faintly on the moist sea-wind from beyond the ridge and the bay: the unmistakable gabbling, barking, hallooing cry—almost speech—of breloons on a fresh trail. The taut feeling in his middle got worse. Breloons unleashed there, within the inner Fiefdom, meant a slave escape. And that meant trouble for the Freed Folk around the fringe.

There was a stir behind him, and the strip of moonlight fell on an eleven-year-old face. "What is it, Dad?"

"Breloons, just over the ridge. Wake Sis and your mother!"

Murno moved about the dark room, donning his leather garments, short boots, scabbarded hunting-knife, and quiver of arrows; slung his bow over his shoulder. Klayr—up and dressed as efficiently as he—whispered, "Shall I make you some sandwiches?"

"No. My story'll be that I'm just out on a short food-hunt. Stay close to the cottage and act as if nothing were up. If you see any neighbors, just tell them I heard breloons. Keep an eye out for geehawks—in a case like this, they might dive and slash with their talons."

"All right," she said listlessly, "but I wish you didn't have to go!"

"I'm the closest," he said. "It's my responsibility to find out what's going on."

Though this was early summer, the wind was cool

enough to make him shiver as he forced his way through the knee-high grass. He could no longer hear anything from beyond the ridge, nor could he smell anything but pepperwood and pine. He paused as he reached the trees, and looked back. The moon now lit only half the eastern slope, leaving the level valley floor a dark ghostly place where he could barely make out the cottage.

He reached the top of the ridge while the moon still lingered over the bay inlet called the Golden Gate. He moved northward to where he had a favorite lookout tree—not on the highest hill; that would be too conspicuous. Old Fief Kokiel, who'd given Murno his freedom years ago, didn't object if the Free Folk crossed the ridge now and then so long as they kept clear of Kokiel's paying guests—but this was different.

The mist had vanished in the early sun. The western slopes, the gently-tilted land between them and the bay (thickly wooded, though shards of ancient ruins showed here and there), and the bay itself, sparkled under a clear sky. The Gaddyl liked plenty of rain to keep things green, but they liked their days spanking bright, and they'd arranged things that way in certain parts of the world.

He peered across the bay toward the Golden Gate.

To the south of the narrow inlet, the old ruins of, so legend said, a human city, were still partly masked by fog. North of the inlet, the big mountain mass loomed above the haze. That was where the Citadel and barracks and armories and inns and hotels were clustered. He could see dots in the sky over it—aircars—but their pattern wasn't ordinary, nor did the usual pleasure-boats move about the bay. So, the trouble wasn't over.

The pre-dawn chase had gone north, but the sky was empty there—no geehawks circled. Or—wait—were those geehawks, so far north he could barely see them?

No. They moved more like vultures. He stared that way unhappily. They could be circling over some animal carcass, of course, but he'd have to go make sure.

He climbed down from his tree, wishing the jays and squirrels wouldn't make so much fuss, and went north along the ridge. The pine-needles here made a flooring that wouldn't show his bootprints too clearly. He reached a fold of the ridge and started down the steep ravine, where blackberry patches grew, toward a secret cache he kept. Presently there was a small spring, and after that he walked in the water, careful not to leave prints.

The cache—in a jumble of rocks—consisted of a pair of overboots, made not too long ago from a bearskin. He drew them on. Now, so far as scent trails were concerned, he was a bear.

On the way north, he constructed several trail-puzzles. Toward mid-morning he found the track of the breloons. They'd been running all out, straight along the ridges. He paused warily: What kind of a fool would flee in a straight line like that?

He descended the slope a little and took his own way.

During the rest of the morning he saw no aircars and heard nothing. He did, though, see single geehawks, circling high up. He was careful to stay out of their sight. If one of them swooped, the tiny radio it wore around its neck would advertise the fact to some Gaddyl monitor.

Before noon he crossed the breloons' trail again.

The hills had flattened, here, to a wide tilted apron that sloped down to a northern lobe of the bay. The ground was soggy, so he had to be careful. He invested more time than he liked in circling north to get into thick brush, then very cautiously approached the spot where the vultures circled. Once, a movement ahead of him made him crouch, pulse quickening, but it was only an old she-bear herding two cubs somewhere.

Finally he parted a last screen of brush and saw what the vultures were after.

The escapee, this one at least, had been a Norm (a nonmutant human), young and lithe-limbed. His last hours clearly hadn't been pleasant. The desperate flight along the hills must have been an agony in itself, but it was only a prelude. Obviously, the breloons' handlers must have been present when the huge mutant-baboon tracking-beasts caught their prey, else he'd have been torn to bits. But, though his face was an awful shredded mess, he'd still been alive when the Gaddyl strung him up by his feet, with his arms bound behind him. Murno could tell that by the amount of blood below the corpse.

7

One of the vultures, newly landed, waddled to the corpse, stretched out an ugly neck, seized a bit of flesh, and tugging it loose, set the corpse to swinging and turning gently on its rope. The stench of blood was sickening: the breloon-smell clung to the place. Murno yearned to be away from it, but he stayed to study every detail.

The slave's tunic told him nothing; a single loose gray garment that left arms and legs bare. Short boots, though—they meant the slave had been in the field when he made his break. Probably he'd been with some sporting-party southward along the bay, and had run straight north. Why? Even a young slave with no woodsmanship at all should have sense enough to take to the streams and to construct trail puzzles.

Unless he were deliberately drawing the pursuit north. The leaden feeling in Murno's stomach grew. Clearly, the hunt was still on, and the others would have taken a different direction. The most likely one, considering the terrain, was toward the scattered community of Freed Folk east of the hills.

It was one of the things Murno and his neighbors dreaded, for it posed a terrible dilemma.

Well, he'd done his duty—now the job was to get back to his family.

He took a different route home, disposing of the bearskin overboots where they wouldn't be found, and coming out at the head of his own small valley. He walked down it openly, fairly sure he'd left no trail that could be followed. The day wore on. Late in the afternoon, he reached the bend a couple of miles above his cottage. Murno took a deer trail paralleling the creek. One more turn, and home would be in sight.

Suddenly he stopped, crouching slightly. It was too quiet.

CHAPTER II: THE NEW FIEF

The man-sized, deep-chested beasts came in two groups from the willow thicket, fanning out to encircle him. He controlled his instincts and stood still—obviously they

8

hadn't been set on his trail, therefore they wouldn't attack without provocation. Still, one wrong move. . . . For a moment they darted about, trampling a circle of grass so they'd have free movement, then they squatted, grinning and gibbering and showing him their three-inch fangs and making small quick sideward movements of their heads, which was their way of insulting him. Carefully, he turned his head to survey the sky. No geehawks aloft. That meant the breloons' masters were close by.

The aircar—a four-seated open model, with a hairless sallow-skinned mutant-human slave piloting, and with two Gaddyl in the back seats, came beelining over the hills from the east. The geehawks—huge hunting-birds mutated from eagles by the Gaddyl, generations ago—were perched, six of them, on the car's rear rail. Their fierce eyes stared unblinkingly at Murno.

He looked at the two aliens, and gave an involuntary start that brought the breloons to their feet, snarling anew. He knew both the Gaddyl.

Earth's alien rulers were about the size of men, a little broader of hip and narrower of shoulder. Their hands and feet were partially webbed; the skin hairless, with a pebbly light-green texture. The necks were long and thick and quite flexible, so that they could bend from the vertical like stovepipes, to bring the egg-shaped heads to bear, nose forward, upon Murno. The faces were flat-featured, without external ears. There was a dorsal crest, from the back of the head to the waist, hanging limp now, so that a Gaddyl upper garment must be backless or very roomy. Gaddyl were not particularly graceful-looking when they sat or stood. Swimming, they were grace itself.

Nictating membranes slid for a moment across the older alien's eyes. "It has been many years, Murno. That is quite a beard you have now." His English was like Murno's.

"Many years, Your Eminence Oory." Murno inclined his head as one must, and kept his face calm, but inside him a new worry began to gnaw. Oory was Chief-At-Arms to Fief Kokiel. Why, then, did the ride with Kokiel's heir, Guddun? There had been rumors that Kokiel was failing.

The young alien spoke, in Gaddyl, contemptuously. "So you are Murno."

9

"Yes, Young Sir." Murno answered, of course, in the alien tongue, as addressed.

"I am told," Guddun said, "that you once touched me."

Murno stifled the resentment that began to grow in him. "It was unavoidable, My Lord. The jeel was upon us, and you were too young to run."

Guddun said coldly, "I have heard the story, and I am not flattered. Do you know you are the only non-mutant human in the history of this Fiefdom who has touched a Gaddyl and been pardoned?"

"I know that, Young Sir." Murno thought it best not to add that he'd expected death at the time. Though more than fourteen years had passed, the dilemma was still sharp in his memory. He could have sneaked away and let the jeel—an off-world beast more like a huge, very agile reptile than anything else—kill the alien child. No one would have known he'd been near. To touch the child, much less pick it up and run with it, was automatically punishable by death. He was not sure he'd make the same choice today, even though Kokiel had broken the rule, pardoned him, and given him his freedom.

Guddun was saying, "A stupid decision on my father's part. My Chief-At -Arms here"— nodding toward Oory— "thinks I should be grateful that you saved my life. That, also, is stupid. Between Gaddyl and slave there can be no such feeling. There is no common plane of existence. Do you understand that?"

Murno struggled to control himself. "I do indeed, Young Sir." He hesitated. "Your manner of referring to His Eminence Oory . . . may one presume that Fief Kokiel is dead?"

Guddun said carelessly, "My father died twice ten days ago. He had lived a full life. If you're thinking there'll be less laxity now, you're correct. No more crossing the ridge, for one thing." He turned absently, and, with a light stick he carried, rapped on the hairless skull of the mutant slave. "This one understands his position. You—have you heard the story of how Murno saved me?"

"I have heard, Master."

"What would you have done in his place?"

"Why, the same as he, of course, Master."

"And you would not think it unjust to be executed?"

"It is not forbidden, Master, for slaves of my mutation to touch Gaddyl."

"Of course not, fool! Suppose you were a Norm like Murno. Would you have saved me, and would you think it unjust to die?"

The slave turned a puzzled look toward Guddun. "Of course I would have, Master, and of course I would not think it unjust."

Guddun gave Oory a malicious look, displaying his many small pointed teeth, then turned to Murno. "Where have you been today?"

"Up this valley, Young Sir, hunting."

"Is that bow your only weapon?"

"Except for the knife, My Lord."

"What were you hunting?"

"I thought I might take a young pig."

"And did you?"

"No, Young Sir. The game seems to be frightened away."

Guddun grinned. "Did you hear the breloons last night?"

Murno said carefully, "I heard a chase, west of the ridge. I guessed a slave was being pursued. For that reason, I did not leave my valley."

"And that's all you guessed? You did not become curious?"

"We ems, My Lord, take care to avoid such things."

"You had better. How many ems live within a day's walk of here?"

"Not more than thirty families, Young Sir. Mine is the only cottage in this valley."

"We noticed that, fool, when we set the breloons down. Now, I'll remind you of one condition of your freedom: if at any time you encounter a runaway slave, you are to capture him and return him to us. If you cannot take him alive, bring his head. You understand?"

"Yes, My Lord."

"And if you should ever see or hear of anything stolen from us, you are to send word to us."

"Yes." So that was it! There was contraband. Murno glanced at Oory. The nictating membranes covered half the older alien's eyes in embarrassment.

11

Guddun shouted a command to the breloons and grunted a word to the pilot. The car lifted, swung around, and zoomed for the western ridge. The beasts, reluctantly, broke their circle and went bobbing away through the grass, in their deceptive gait.

As the aircar topped the ridge, the geehawks launched off and flapped for altitude. The hunt beyond the ridge was being resumed. Murno started home, full of dread.

The window shutters were closed. Klayr unbarred the door when he came in sight. She clutched him for a moment in silent relief, while the youngsters, at their window watch-posts, eyed him gravely. Klayr let him go. "There was an aircar, and geehawks, and we heard breloons up the creek!"

"I met them. They're after at least one more slave. They've already caught one."

"Oh," she said, "I hope he doesn't come near us. I can't help feeling that way!"

"Don't you think I feel the same way? But if he does, we'll have to face up to it. Things are bad enough anyway. Kokiel's dead, and Guddun's Fief."

She looked at him without real comprehension. She'd been born free, the daughter of an em, and had never known Kokiel or Guddun. Klayr knew slave-life only by hearsay. "Do you mean we may have to leave here?"

"It's very possible. Anyway, we'll have to be on guard for the next few days. Do we have enough wood and water?"

Gaje said, "I got it in this morning, Dad."

Later, while Klayr worked by the light of oil lamps, patiently putting tiny perforations in a new leather garment, and Gaje helped his nine-year-old sister with her reading lessons, Murno sat listlessly braiding a new bow-string from threads. Guddun, obviously, would turn the area inside out to find the rest of the runaways.

It was hard to contemplate leaving now. He'd worked so hard to build the sturdy cottage and make it comfortable. He planted fruit trees and vegetables. Life was—had been—easy enough here on the protected fringe of the Fiefdom. Where would they go? This patch of green

12

country wasn't very big. Not many miles east was the edge of the vast Sack Toe Valley that ran most of the length of the vaguely-defined area called Kalf. That valley was a wide wild plain, grassy enough to support great herds of bovines which were preyed upon by various carnivores—including the lions that were one of the favorite game animals of Gaddyl sportsmen from off-planet. There was no Fiefdom there, no humans except for a few renegades. Northward, far beyond the straits at the head of the bay, were two other Fiefdoms on fresh-water lakes. Each tolerated ems, but strange ones arriving would be suspect. Hundreds of miles south was another on the coast. In Murno's time as a slave—he'd gotten around, being in Kokiel's personal service—that had been a harsh Fiefdom.

Of course, there were the Sierra Norms—or so rumor and legend claimed—whose ancestors had never been conquered, but had taken refuge in the snow country, and to this day held some civilization—more, at least, than the various Wild Folk, normal or mutant. But they were beyond the Sack Toe Valley—not to mention the mysterious, half-legendary Blue Mutants who dwelled among the wooded Sierra foothills, and who, some said, were cannibals.

Or the land beyond the Sierras—strange wild country, some lush, some dry as it had been before the coming of the Gaddyl, teeming with game and inhabited by Wild Folk. Murno, as a slave, had flown over some of it a few times. There were spots that looked livable. But to get to them seemed almost as impossible as getting to some other world.

He might have to stay here and hope.

He glanced at the water-clock, made from a precious glass jar he'd bought years ago. "I suppose we may as well go to bed."

CHAPTER III: "OMHA ABIDES"

Neither he nor Klayr had spoken for an hour, but he knew she too was awake. Certainly, *he* was nowhere near sleep. He felt as if he were in a totally strange place: the bunk felt different, the cottage around him different. The sounds of the valley, familiar as his pulse—muskrats and turtles plopping into the creek; deer wading; an owl's sad observation; the soughing of night wind over the grass—all were changed. He kept imagining more furtive sounds.

It must have been near midnight when he heard something definitely furtive. He rolled over, felt for the scabbard hanging on the bedpost and came to his feet, ears straining.

A small slapping sound came from the creek, repeated twice, then twice more. Murno hurried to the rear window and carefully separated shutter slats.

He put his mouth near the crack and spoke disjointedly so possible geehawks wouldn't recognize his human speech. "Who?"

The answer was similarly cautious. "Joe. Kenth's boy. Bad trouble!"

The knot in Murno's stomach drew tighter. Kenth lived in the next valley east, and two miles south. "Where's Kenth?"

"Gone warn neighbors. We all have to leave!"

Murno stood silent for a minute, hoping it could all be a dream, then, suddenly, made his decision. "Can you wait there?"

"Yes. Hurry!" The distress was thick in the twelve-year-old's voice.

Klayr was up now, and at Murno's shoulder. He told her in a tense whisper, "Get the kids up and start packing as we've rehearsed. I'll get the deerskins."

Beyond one sharp intake of breath she didn't protest, but hurried silently to the kitchen. Murno dressed, went to the living-room wall nearest the creek, and carefully opened the door of a lean-to closet built onto the cottage. That closet, besides being a storage place, was the secret exit. He took from a shelf the rolled-up deerskins—including one for Joe—and felt about for the quivers of arrows and Gaje's light bow. He hauled everything to the table, slung his own bow over his shoulder and strapped on three of the quivers. Gaje would take the fourth. Now the backpack went on over the other stuff. Then he slipped on the biggest of the deerskins, like a cloak, with the forelegs tied around his neck. He could hear Klayr and the children at their own tasks.

14

Before he let them out he tied a deerskin over each one's back. The skins were awkward, over knapsacks, but they might fool geehawks.

There was mud in the bottom of the tunnel, but that had to be ignored. He pushed aside the earth-covered square of boards, cautiously poking up his head in a clump of willows. All right so far. He hauled himself out, then turned to help Sis. They made a lot more noise than he liked, but nothing came to investigate.

Joe was squatting in moon-shadow. Beside him on the ground rested a full knapsack. Murno handed him the rolled-up deerskin. "Camouflage. Want me take big pack?"

"Better!" Joe hoisted it, grunted, and passed it to Murno. "I'll take yours. This got Gaddyl things in it. Runaway brought them to Dad."

Murno sighed. No time now to feel sorry for himself. It was beginning to look very much as if the slave break had not been anything impulsive. It looked planned. His mind tried to resist certain other thoughts but failed. Slowly, he asked, "Message?"

"Yes. I don't understand it. 'Sierra Norms. Omha Abides!' "

Murno let out his breath wearily. He didn't have to look in the knapsack—whatever it held, besides Joe's food and extra clothes, would be worth the plot. Neither did he ponder why he was chosen. Years ago, as a young slave, he'd made the wild, secret vows. And now he was being called to turn—someone, possibly one of the escapees, knew of him; knew he'd be more familiar with Gaddyl instruments or weapons than almost any em; knew he possessed—if anyone did—the woodsmanship to elude the search.

Why, he thought angrily, should he honor those long-forgotten vows? "Omha" was somebody else's myth. Why jeopardize his family on a fool's errand? The thing to do was contact the Fiefdom diplomatically, and . . .

Suddenly, he cursed to himself. With Guddun in the chair?

Slowly, he untied his deerskin to swap packs with Joe. The unknown planner had timed things too well. He whispered sullenly, "We'll wade up-creek a ways, then climb the east slope on all fours. We'll head north, loop

15

back a time or two, and try to get to a hiding-place I know. Then as soon as there's a rainy night we'll go east. Keep together unless something bad happens—in which case, scatter."

He led the way until he heard deer; then paused and made a cougar sound. The deer bolted for the eastern slope. No geehawks. Good! He led the way on all fours, following the deer. Once he heard broad wings whisper overhead, but the geehawk, used to the deer, didn't pause. He reached the fringe of trees, stood up, and took off his deerskin. "Roll them up and carry them."

The mid-morning sun was hot. These hills—only a few miles from his own valley—were noticeably drier, and less wooded. Still, the ravine he turned up was choked with brush except in its creeklet. There was enough water to hide scent.

Halfway up, he forced a way into the brush, the others filing behind him. It was an hour's struggle, but before noon he reached the place he wanted.

Just below the brow of a hill was a large blackberry patch surrounding a rock outcropping. It looked as if the rocks couldn't be reached without hacking a way in, but there was a route. More than once he'd holed up there to spy on cougars, bear, or other beasts he didn't want to tangle with. He got Klayr and the youngsters in with no more damage than a few scratches. Beneath the great rocks was a cubbyhole where stone had fallen away sometime in the past and was now thoroughly screened by the vines. It wasn't going to be excessively roomy for the five of them, but it was the best place he knew—it had the virtue that he could look out upon the hillside and down the ravine, see over the hills to the west and to either side. "Let's make the best beds we can." That occupied half an hour. Sis lay down and was asleep at once.

Murno stowed the knapsacks and other gear, except for the knapsack Joe had brought. That, he set on the ground in the best light. He stared at it for a few minutes, reluctant to open it. Finally he sighed. "We're safe here for the moment, and we can talk. Joe, tell me about the escapee."

Joe—a thin, angular redhead, tall for his age—sat down against a rock and drew his thin leather-clad knees up

16

before him. "He came to our place an hour after dark. He knew who we were, and who you were. He told us Guddun was Fief now, and that things would be bad, and that he and two others had rushed through a plan they had because they thought it was now or never. There's a gadget in there that they stole from an aircar, and another they got out of a security vault at the citadel—something a Gaddyl hunting party had found somewhere. Then there's a handgun."

Murno slowly undid the hasps. The handgun alone was enough to set off a furious search. If it reached any of the Wild Folk, in the vast areas away from any Fiefdom, it could be a real threat to Gaddyl hunting parties—and a Fief couldn't afford to have mishaps befall his guests. The competition for business was too keen. He drew it out and turned it over slowly in his hands. He'd held such weapons before, but not for a long time. There was a grip that fit the hand naturally, with a trigger for the forefinger and a sliding stud under the thumb, to change settings. The power unit was a finger-sized rod that thrust into the grip from below and locked in place—and popped out automatically when exhausted. The barrel was an inch thick and five inches long, of greenish metalloplast that ordinary tool steels would barely scratch. Inside, Murno knew, were complex windings that hurled a bolt of energy in a far-reaching pencil or a shorter-range cone, depending on how the weapon was set.

It was considered unsporting to turn such a weapon on wild game. Of course, a handgun was good to have if the game got the upper hand.

He set the weapon down gingerly, and reached into the pack for one of the instruments.

This was the size of a medium potato, oval and bulging on one side, flat on the other. There were holes in the flat side for fastening-screws; and distortion of these hinted that the instrument had been pried off something. "Is this the one that was stolen from an aircar?"

"That's what the escapee said."

Murno frowned over it. He'd never seen such an article in an aircar. Still, it looked like something to be temporarily mounted; and in any case, he hadn't been in an aircar since his manumission.

17

He put the thing down and rummaged around for the other.

This was more puzzling than the first. It was a half-sphere, two inches in diameter, with a small rounded piece of dark glass set in the top. The glass might be a lens, he thought, except for its near-opacity. Around the hemisphere, near the base, was a barely visible band, as if it had been painted once but faded. The metal was dull and scratched; only the glass looked new. He had the feeling the thing had lain out in the weather for a long time.

Almost certainly, it was no Gaddyl artifact—they wouldn't use stainless steel for such a thing, when metalloplast was superior and so much lighter. An ancient human device, then—they were found occasionally. But this one didn't look as old as most.

He transferred the things to his own knapsack. Then he managed to nap a little.

Around mid-afternoon he came awake to the distant sound of breloons.

He lay as far forward in the vines as he could, chin resting on his hands, waiting like some animal gone to earth. The tracking was headed this way.

Geehawks soared into sight, circling ever closer, heads swinging from side to side in a search ahead of the breloons. Before long, the latter would reach the mouth of the thicketed ravine.

Suddenly, one of the birds swooped, and others joined it. He went limp with relief. So they weren't on his trail. That was a selfish reaction, but he couldn't help it. He watched the birds flap in mad tight circles, screaming, like seagulls after a beached fish, heard the clamor of the breloons take on a more urgent note.

Murno caught only glimpses at first of the man who turned up the ravine, but he recognized the gray slave-tunic and field boots. He'd never seen the man before. Helplessly, he watched the desperate climb and saw the gasping agony in the middle-aged face.

What if the breloons just happened to sniff Murno's own trail? What if?

The man's strength gave out. Limply, he fell, slid, grasped at bushes and checked himself. He lay panting for

18

a moment, then summoned from somewhere the strength to haul himself to his feet, turn, and draw a knife.

The brown bobbing shapes were boiling into the ravine now. Geehawks were diving at the man's face. He warded them off with his left hand—Murno saw blood well from a finger—and took what shelter he could in the brush. Murno felt someone squirm up beside him, and darting a look, saw Joe. "Is that the slave you saw?"

"N-no."

The breloons spotting the quarry, shrilled their blood-lust, and bunched for the attack. One leaped in. The knife flashed, but the beast was already away—and another was almost to the man's leg before the knife was back in position.

An aircar zoomed into sight. Gaddyl shouted at the beasts—they wanted this fugitive alive. The breloons hesitated. Deliberately, the slave threw himself at them.

The Gaddyl shouted frantically, and a handgun beam —narrowed—slashed at the man's right shoulder. He screamed and went down, the knife clattering in the ravine. But again he squirmed upright and jumped, screaming curses at the breloons.

This time there was no restraining them. The brown forms, clamoring, swarmed over the gray-clad figure.

It took the handlers five minutes to get the beasts off the corpse and send them bobbing down-ravine. The Gaddyl voices reached Murno. One said, "Two out of three. But Guddun will be hellish mad that we didn't take him alive!"

The other made the equivalent of a shrug. "We need not tell him the precise order of events. In any case, there's plenty more two-legged game to keep him occupied now."

"True. Let's heave this carrion aboard and be off."

Murno lay limp and ill, watching the aircar depart. Behind him, Sis was sobbing quietly. He could smell the breloons still, and blood and scorched flesh.

The south wind came at dusk, and with it the rain Murno hoped for. Now there was no danger of leaving scent-trails; no worry about geehawks. But he had to cross some very hilly country in the dark.

He roused the family and got them started. While the last light held, he was all right—he could still recognize the terrain. After that the trek became a nightmare. The moon above the clouds gave enough light so he could avoid treetrunks, but the footing was treacherous. Time and again he stumbled. Sometimes he caught himself, sometimes he sprawled. Once he fell against rough bark and tasted blood from a split lip. He pressed stubbornly on, knowing he must cover many miles before dawn. There was no way to tell direction except by the slant of the rain—and if the wind shifted, that wouldn't be reliable.

They stopped five or six times to rest and eat. On one of those occasions they were on a slope rising northward which he knew must be the south shoulder of the highest hill in the vicinity of Bay. After that the trek was generally downhill, but by now Sis was barely able to keep moving. He decided, sometime before dawn, to risk a full hour's stop. The rain had slackened, but it might last.

The sky was already fading when they descended a last hill and peered out over rolling oak-dotted country. Murno hesitated. He wanted to be away from this margin before the weather broke. "Do you and the kids feel up to spending the day in a tree?"

Klayr said wearily, "If we have to."

He found a very shallow ravine draining east, fairly well lined with oaks; urged them along it for about two miles.

He chose a pair of oaks with interlacing foliage. "I'll toss a rope over a limb," he told Gaje, "and I want you to shinny up and tie it where I show you. We'll need a rope ladder we can pull up after us, and some horizontal ropes to tie the deerskins to for hammocks."

By an hour after sun-up, the day was sparkling-clear. Sis

20

was sleeping like a statue, and the others were at least napping. Murno, ready enough for sleep, felt he'd better climb high in the tree and survey what he could of the surroundings.

The hills they'd left were disappointingly close. Eastward, not more than a mile, was some kind of waterway lined with willows, towered over by a few tall elms. All he could see beyond the waterway (or north, or south) was gently rolling country speckled with oaks. The grass, except under the jealous oaks, was fairly lush, though not equal to that in his own valley. There were clumps of flowers he couldn't name. Larks were fluting in the grass; the purest, coolest sound he could imagine. Insects made a haze. Not far from his tree, a jackrabbit went toward the waterway in high watchful bounds. The smells were rising now—succulent grass-odor, flower perfumes, the astringent smell of oaks. He thunked curiously with his forefinger at an oakball. Not part of the tree, he recalled reading somewhere, but an excrescence caused by some insect parasite.

There were plentiful signs of grazing, and under the trees out of this shallow ravine, dung where bovines had stood in the shade. He didn't particularly welcome that sign. Bovines brought sportsmen; also, four-footed predators.

Tentatively, he planned to head a little south of east, skirting the slough country where several rivers—including the Sack Toe from the north and the San Wah Keen from the south—found a thousand twisting ways to the bay. Gaddyl went there for swimming and fishing. If he could reach the San Wah Keen and cross it, he'd be in wilder country, less policed by Fiefdom Bay (though parties from Bay, as well as other Fiefdoms, went there for big game).

He'd have to be wary of some of that game. That was jeel country, among other things—it was there he'd saved the child Guddun's life, so many years ago.

Klayr stirred on her hammock, and he watched her for a moment. Would it be possible to find some place to leave her and the youngsters, while he made his perilous trek? Some waterway too small to attract Gaddyl, but with adequate cover, and with fish, small game, and possibly fowl's eggs? Or—one of the ancient ruins that still poked out of the land here and there? Renegades were said to find

21

shelter occasionally in cave-like remains of old concrete buildings.

Two events during the day put an end to such thinking.

First—about midmorning—geehawks appeared over the fringe of the hills he'd left. Several aircars cruised north and south, holding the birds to their pattern and adding Gaddyl eyes to the search. The implication was clear: there were still fugitives—some of Murno's neighbors—at large; and Guddun intended to seal them into the patch of hills east of Bay.

Second—near noon—a geehawk-and-breloon search swept up the waterway a mile to the east. Murno, at times, could faintly hear the tracking-beasts; but even if he couldn't, the way the birds circled and the way the three or four aircars behaved would have told him there were breloons.

"Is that the San Wah Keen?"

Murno started at Joe's quiet question. Carefully, he moved nearer the youngster. "No. The San Wah Keen's a real river, twenty miles or so east."

Joe squinted at the hawks, now moving to the south. "Why are they scouting a small creek?"

"That's what *I've* been wondering. Someone may have got to the straits at the north of the bay, and headed inland along the waterways. Or—Guddun may simply suspect someone's made it out of the hills, and be trying to pick up a trail." He shifted in the tree-crotch, trying to find more comfort. "I hope Oory's not in charge of the hunt. He'd be a lot shrewder than Guddun."

Joe glanced at him, then stared back at the creek.

Murno guessed what might be in the boy's mind. "Your father," he said quietly, "is a woodsman, and he knows the hills almost as well as I do. There's a good chance he got the family away all right."

Joe turned to him slowly. "Do you think I'll ever know?"

Murno couldn't say yes honestly. Instead, he asked, "Are you willing to throw in with us? You'll be heading farther away. But I don't see how you can stay here."

There were the beginnings of tears in the boy's eyes. "I've got to go with you. Dad told me to. He . . . doesn't

22

want me caught, because I know where those things in your knapsack are headed."

Murno had no reply to that either; and he was glad Joe didn't stare at him too long. The implication wasn't pleasant: Kenth didn't intend himself, or Joe's mother, to be taken alive either.

There was no rain that night, so, on crossing the creek, Murno constructed trail puzzles. Then he pushed on cross-country, keeping as much as possible to the cover of oaks. He didn't like this at all; leaving plain trails in the grass; travelling in strange country, with the rising moon full in his eyes.

There were other small waterways to cross. One, for a while, turned eastward; he followed it gratefully. Then he had to strike out through grass again. "I think we'd better not walk in single file or a straight line. Spread out a little, and wander a few feet to the sides, as cattle would."

An hour after that, he was heading for a big oak when he sensed presences in the black shadow under it. "Hold up!"

He peered into the blackness. How could the moon be so bright, and leave such dense shadows? "Move down-wind, very slowly," he whispered. He felt for an arrow; got his bow in hand; moved laterally, staying between family and oak.

A vague bulk shifted in the blackness. He kept circling to the north, slowly. After a while he caught fresh bovine smell. He felt a little relief, but not much. So far as he knew, there were only the short-horned cattle in this part of the valley, but they could be dangerous enough when they felt threatened. It would take an exceptional arrow-shot to stop a bull.

But they got by safely. After that he was more circumspect about the oaks he approached.

They stopped, ate sparingly, rested, and went on. The moon gradually obliged by moving west.

But sometime after midnight Klayr whispered, "I'm sure there's something following us!"

Murno peered back into the moonlight. They'd just passed under an oak. Did something pause there now, in

23

the shade? If so, they had a fifty-yard lead. He looked around for another oak, small enough so Klayr and the youngsters could shinny up in a pinch. "Move on ahead, slowly."

In the shelter of the small oak, he paused a full ten minutes, looking back. Nothing. "We may as well rest here a while anyway, and watch."

He allowed fifteen minutes, then urged them on. Now, though, he paid attention to both flanks as well as ahead and behind—but, mostly, he kept a surreptitious watch downwind.

It was half an hour before he glimpsed it—a furtive pale shape in the moonlight, a full hundred yards to their left.

He stopped, midriff knotting. A lioness—not a cougar—but the larger feline that might be very dangerous if hungry. He reached for his bow, then hesitated. He had the Gaddyl handgun in his pack. This far out, could he risk using it? The burst of static would register on a wide radio-band. He could be far from this spot before an aircar got here from any Fiefdom—but suppose there were a flying monitor somewhere near?

The lioness was, possibly, an immediate threat and one not to be faced with arrows. Slowly, he reached for the fastenings of the pack.

The rest of the night, he walked with the alien gun in his hand. But he saw no more of the feline. She had, perhaps, only been curious.

They spent the next day beneath a large oak—out of sight of any cattle, in case of casual hunting-parties. Twice he saw aircars cruising high up, and late in the afternoon he heard rifle shots somewhere south. He waited nervously, fearing that bovines might stampede this way. None did.

The next night they had a real scare that turned into a puzzling incident.

They were travelling down a nearly-dry creek that ran east—a tributary, he supposed, of the San Wah Keen—and came within sight of some jagged old ruins that thrust up above the willows. The moon—past full, now—was medium-high in the east; therefore, he was going cautiously.

Murno paused, trying to assess the stretch between them and the ruins. There was an odd feel about the place—

perhaps it was the absence of the small life that should have been stirring.

Then the breeze shifted and he caught just a hint of a rank, carrion-like odor.

He crouched in sudden terror. That was the jeel-smell! From what direction did it come—or did it cling to the area? The ruins—like an outcropping of great rocks—could be a lair. But what was a jeel doing on this side of the San Wah Keen? For that matter, was the place dry enough for a jeel?

That, he told himself nervously, was the jeel's problem. He didn't think he could be wrong about the smell.

If one were near, it was aware of them—jeels were nocturnal, with senses incredibly keen; the more effective, perhaps, for having been transplanted from their home world. Very slowly, he reached for the Gaddyl weapon.

There was a faint susurration which he recognized as an intake of breath via big armored nostrils. He whirled toward the sound—behind him—and leaped clear of his family. He heard the willows crush; aimed the handgun frantically—but before the jeel could charge, there came from off to the side an arresting high-pitched call—a single musical tone, sung by a clear human voice. Even as he felt his own muscles go oddly rigid, he heard the jeel's startled croak. Then the voice broke into a cascade of quick liquid notes—five or six down the scale; and odd shift of key; two more notes in a trill, then sudden silence as jarring as the sound it followed. The jeel rose immensely from behind the willows, crashed across the creek in two mighty bounds, and hurtled off northward—fluting in a mad, frantic way.

Murno, astounded and still unable to move, listened to the massive flight. It diminished into the distance. When it was gone, he was suddenly free to move. Shakily, he turned the other way.

But now there came only a faint, far-away answer to the tenor voice, and after that, nothing. Presently he crept across the creek and parted the willows to peer out. The grass, with no sign of a trail in it, rippled in a breeze.

Eventually—as shaken by the queer stasis that had gripped him as by the encounter with a jeel—he managed to say, "Come on!" He led the way out of the creek and far around the ancient ruins, which did indeed reek of jeel.

There wasn't much more said until a line of trees—tall ones—loomed ahead. He stopped, studying them. "That's the river. I've been thinking we might stop here a day or two. How's the food holding out?"

Klayr said, "Two more snacks."

CHAPTER V: THE SAN WAH KEEN

The tree-platforms—a half-day's work—were in a huge elm far enough within the bottomland to be invisible from outside, but still a hundred yards from the river proper. Here, a lacework of channels—some dry, some pondy, some still flowing—chopped the bottomland into a multiplicity of islands, even the smaller of which were choked with willows, elderberries, and such. In this shady subworld, even in the daytime, muskrats, raccoons, cottontails, and a dozen other species of small life scurried about. Murno even saw one gray fox. Birds were everywhere. Surely, there'd be bobcats at night.

He got the family installed. "You can try fishing, but don't go near the main river. Gaje, you and Joe shoot cottontails if you can, and try to find a few big rocks for a cooking-place. I'm going to scout around for better meat, and see what signs there are of Gaddyl. I'll be back before dark."

He was careful when he neared the river. There were waterfowl about, though, indicating that this stretch wasn't frequented by Gaddyl. The brown stream, seventy or eighty yards wide now, flowed fairly fast in a channel that twisted but remained near the east bank of the bottomland —leaving rootage on that side only for willows and brush. The dirt bank was a dozen feet high, collapsed in places— showing, in those places, plenty of hoof-marks.

He noted where eggs might be found and then retreated from the main channel and went upstream.

There was nothing different—no deer or pig signs—for a mile and a half.

And then a narrow fork of the main channel barred his way.

He hesitated, studying the point of land. Island or gore?

The fork looked deep enough so he'd have to swim. Murno listened; glanced at the sun and decided to have a look.

He'd no sooner hauled himself to the opposite bank and through its screen of willows than he felt the strangeness of the place.

Though the ground looked ample there were no elms. Perhaps because the shade was lacking, the small growth was profuse. Elderberries formed solid ranks; apricot trees struggled for living-room; almonds reached skyward above thickets. There were crabapples and some fruit trees even he didn't know.

A jay hopped from a branch and planed away, eyeing him silently. He watched it closely. Silence was unlike jays.

Murno pushed on, detouring where necessary, for a ways. He could hear the river on both sides, so probably this was a long slender island. He was about to turn back when the south breeze brought him a familiar smell. Pigs! He slipped his bow off his shoulders, selected an arrow, and advanced quietly.

The pigs were in a mud-wallow in the shade of a tree something like a magnolia, but with no blossoms and with a denser crop of leaves. There was one boar mature enough to show the high foreshoulders, razor-back, shaggy hair, and tusks that might mislead some people to think he was a different species. Murno didn't want to tangle with that fellow. There were four sows of various ages, and a dozen young pigs of at least three separate litters. Murno hesitated. He didn't particularly feel like killing any of a social group of this sort. But pork, well cooked, couldn't be surpassed as a supply of meat to carry.

He ran thumb and forefinger along the bowstring to squeeze it dry, nocked the arrow, and held the weapon in his left hand while he looked around for something to throw. He found a chunk of broken limb, hefted it, then paused to study the game-trails around the wallow. He didn't want the startled swine bolting toward him.

The only two ways out of the wallow were on opposite sides of the large-limbed tree, twisting into dense brush beyond. Good enough. He moved a few steps to improve his angle, then tossed the chunk of wood in a high arc.

The missile came down inches from one of the sows,

27

making a loud plop and scattering mud. The pigs erupted in a bedlam of grunts and squeals, and were on their feet and moving. Murno, bow drawn, waited while most of them gained solid ground and flashed into the brush—including the boar and the larger sows. There were four pigs still struggling to gain footing. He swung the bow to lead the one he'd chosen, and was about to let fly—when the pig suddenly froze.

Murno stood in a crouch, eyes darting about. What had the pig seen? Then—the tableau lasted only a second—he realized that the animal was facing the trunk of the large-leaved tree, toward which it had happened to bolt.

The pig darted aside, toward one of the trails, and Murno released the arrow. The pig let out a squeal like a siren, leaped once, fell kicking. It died quickly.

Skin prickling a little, Murno walked slowly around the wallow. Before going near the pig, he looked hard at the base of the tree, thinking the pig might have seen a snake.

But pigs, he reminded himself, don't fear small snakes. They eat them.

Well, then, maybe the tree itself was poisonous; or maybe there were deadly insects. Certainly, all the bolting animals had swerved around it. But he saw nothing. Nevertheless, he carried the pig away from the spot to butcher it. Then he headed down-river.

The next day went by without incident. The pork was all cooked and salted and wrapped; there were three-dozen-odd duck-eggs, hardboiled and packed in a bagful of willow leaves; more cooked fish than they'd ever eat before the flavor got high. There was a stewpan full of blackberries, and a few black walnuts from a tree half a mile downstream.

On the third day, an hour after sunrise, Murno was wondering whether they might find a marsh somewhere with rice growing, or find some yams, when Gaje, high in the tree called down furtively, "Dad!"

Murno climbed and followed the pointing finger.

There was no doubt—the bird-shapes to the west were geehawks. They were just spreading out. He clambered down. "We've got to move again!"

"Oh," Klayr said weakly.

Murno began hacking at platform-lashings. "We'll need some of these poles for a raft. You kids hide the rest of them. Get rid of the cooking-stones, too, and everything else we can't carry!"

Klayr—already packing knapsacks—asked in a small voice, "We aren't going to cross the river in daylight, are we?"

"No. We'll. . . ." He fell silent, remembering, from years ago, the country beyond. "We'll hide on an island I found, until night, then cross over." No use telling them that the choice between perils was a hard one.

Evening shadows stretched across the river.

A hawk-and-breloon sweep had gone up the east bank, and Murno could only hope it wouldn't be repeated after dark. He stared across the main channel at the small tributary opposite. If there were water there . . . but it looked dry.

If only he had bearskin overboots for them all, like the ones he'd used so often to hide his own trail. Suddenly he stood up straighter. Pigs smelled as strongly as bears!

He ran to the loaded and waiting raft—seized two empty waterbags. "Stay hidden! I'll be back in a little while!"

Sacrificing caution for speed, he fought through thickets to the hog wallow and scooped the leather bags full of the redolent mud.

When he returned it was Sis who asked, "What's that, Daddy?"

He felt like grinning. "Smelly stuff to smear on our boots after we're across the river."

She leaned forward, sniffed, and made a face. "Ooh."

He tied the bags to the raft and stood thinking. Presently he bent to open his own knapsack, removed the handgun and tied it to his belt with a thong. Then he went to sit down.

Wondering about the night ahead wasn't going to be any fun. The worst, maybe, would be not knowing whether they were starting too soon or too late. But he daren't spend another night here as he'd like to, listening to learn the habits of the animals of the far shore.

The dark river seized upon the raft at once and tried to

wrestle it downstream. Murno was starting two hundred yards above the ravine opposite, to allow for the current. The silt was slippery beneath his bare feet. He was at the downstream side of the raft so he could fight the current, while Klayr and the boys pushed from behind. He stepped into an unexpected hole, floundered, caught his balance and leaned hard against the raft. The water was at his waist now. The boys were already swimming and Klayr was losing her traction too. He saw Sis—on the opposite side of the raft—slip and cling to the raft with one arm while her head went under. His midriff contracted violently. He made a quick move, ready to duck beneath the raft to help her, but she hauled herself up and got the other arm hooked over the edge and she was all right. A surge of emotion swept over him. Through all the terror and exhaustion, she'd hardly whimpered.

The current was shoving irresistibly now. Frantically, he gave up fighting it and, instead, shoved the raft cross-stream with all his strength, swimming with his left arm. He managed a glance toward the shore; saw it sweeping by far too fast. He felt a bludgeon-blow of despair—they'd shoot past the ravine, and God knew where they could beach the raft! But just when he thought they'd failed, he felt silt under his feet. And with a muscle-cracking effort, he checked the raft and drove it ashore.

They clung, exhausted, for a minute; then he forced himself out of the water, limbs feeling like lard, seized a rope at the front, and tugged. The others came to help, and they got the raft out of the water and into the mouth of the ravine.

As he'd feared, the latter was dry.

After a few minutes Joe asked, "What are we going to do about the raft?"

Murno had been pondering that. Still lashed together or dismantled, the hatchet-marked poles couldn't simply be left here, and they couldn't be carried along. He drew his knife and bent to slash at a binding. "We'll take it apart and let the poles go downstream, and hope none of them lodge too close. Then we'll smear our boots with the mud we brought, and start up this ravine. But before long we'll leave it and go cross-country as fast as we can."

Gaje said, "Won't it be easier walking in the ravine?"

"Yes. And for that reason, a lot of animals will be using it that we wouldn't want to meet!"

Obviously, the rising ground they'd reached by morning didn't get much rain in the summer. The soil was dry; the sparse grass already bleached of all green. Oaks grew in the creases only. On slopes that had better-than-ordinary soil, forests of brush grew—strange stunted-looking stuff like dwarf trees, less than five feet tall, with gnarled, dry, splitting trunks the thickness of Murno's wrist, that, astonishingly, supported dense pads of small round leaves forming almost complete cover. The ground between trunks grew nothing else, and there was plenty of room to go on hands and knees if one didn't mind clods, pebbles, beetles and quarter-inch ants.

The only color in the landscape was poppies. Where grass was already straw, clumps of poppies sprouted, their green leaves as unthirsty-looking as if they grew on the moist hills of Bay; the brilliant orange of the blossoms not one whit less spirited for the lack of competition in the landscape. Here and there, the poppies claimed whole hillsides. Strange, Murno thought, how different plants sometimes sorted themselves out, aside from any detectable difference of soil and water and sunlight, as if by treaty.

The scrubby brush was excellent cover, and later in the day they might need it. Just now, geehawks were sweeping southward again this side of the river. They were about to reach the tributary Murno'd started along. He was sure there were breloons on the ground, and they'd pick up the scent of pigs. Would they follow that, making the strategy backfire? It depended on how much intelligent guesswork their handlers made. Anyway, he'd done his best.

He crawled back to the others.

Klayr was awake. "I'm going to the top of this hill and see what I can of the country to the east. I'll be within call," Murno told her.

He found a spot where he had a good view eastward.

The hills undulated higher and higher. There was less of the brush; fewer oaks; more dry grass; more weathered gray rock-outcroppings. Far to the east, in spots—two nights' travel—were dark areas that must be pines. It

31

would be good to be among pines again; though as he remembered, these were a different kind, and the ground drier.

The farthest hills he could see hid the snowy Sierra summit he knew was there.

He rejoined the others again. Nothing to do until night but rest.

The next night, they travelled without incident, and were able to find cover the next day. He saw no geehawks.

Then, the following night, when they were climbing a bare rocky ravine, they met trouble.

The first hint was when a rock clattered down.

Murno, stopped in a crouch, held out an arm to halt the others. He felt for the handgun while he peered into the darkness. At the top of the ravine, huge boulders formed a barrier. Did some beast wait there?

Then he caught the jeel-smell. He turned his head slowly, searching every shadow. In the seconds since the rock had come down, the jeel would have moved. He saw nothing; waited, tense.

The big dark bulk came hurtling suddenly down the left-hand slope—as always, seeming to explode out of a nook far too small for it. The handgun was set for a narrow cone. He raked it back and forth, back again, across the broad head; saw and heard steam erupt and scales fly. The sudden screech was like a siren in his ears. He leaped, trying to put himself in front of the family but was knocked sprawling by a great flailing foreleg. Above the awful screaming of the beast he heard Sis's muffled cry; heard Klayr scream. He tumbled among rocks grabbing for holds; hauled himself to his feet and lurched uphill toward the thrashing beast. He saw Sis, lying limp in the moonlight. Murno hurled himself toward her and pulled her to safety, taking a thump from something.

Long before the creature finished dying, he was carrying Sis—who squirmed and moaned now—up the opposite slope, shouting at the others to follow. Somehow, they reached the top. He thrust the Gaddyl weapon into Klayr's hand. "Take Sis and head straight up-country. The boys and I will make trail puzzles!" Then, as she stood speechless, "Go on! Nothing else lives near a jeel's lair!"

It was half an hour before he overtook her. Sis was sitting up, holding a hand to her cheek. He stared, too out of breath to ask yet, until Klayr said, "She's only bruised."

He allowed ten precious minutes' rest, then picked up Sis and hurried on. He set the hardest pace he could, forcing the others to match it. Two hours more they travelled, until he found a canyon that had a trickle in it, and—pines.

He chose a place where a pine trunk on one side, a boulder on another, gave a sort of shelter. "We'll rest most of the night, then get a start before dawn."

It was incredible that he could stay awake on watch for two hours, but he did, while the boys snored. Then he woke them, told them to watch each other so neither would fall asleep, and stretched himself out on the pine needles. He was asleep immediately.

There was no feeling of time elapsed, but the moon was gone when he was jerked from sleep by Gaje's hand on his shoulder. He hauled himself to a sit, fighting off the drugged dullness that gripped him. "What is it?" he whispered.

"Something between us and the creek!"

Murno's eyes darted in that direction. Blackness. But there was something—a feel, a presence unconsciously heard or deduced. Very slowly, he got to his knees and lowered a hand to push himself upright.

There was a twin pair of gleams three feet or so above where he thought the ground should be. Starlight reflected by a pair of eyes! Not breloons—they'd attack at once. Felines? He could smell none.

He reached for his knife, and the whole area seemed to erupt.

A crushing weight dropped on him. Darkness leaped within darkness. Starlight, filtered through foliage, made tiny patches on pale skin. Strong hands seized him—threw him over on his face and tugged his arms irresistibily behind him to bind them. Klayr screamed. Sis came awake with a cry. The boys' shouts blended with Murno's own. An animal snarled excitedly and a clear tenor voice sang out a single pure note. A beast sniffed and was still. Murno

33

twisted desperately; kicked out and struck something, drew a grunt; then was seized by more hands which lashed his legs too. He strained savagely at the thongs; they cut into his skin but did not break. He went limp suddenly, determined not to waste his strength uselessly.

Several tenor voices began to sing a weird little chant. His muscles jerked and writhed out of control. He shouted in an agony that was not pain. An incredible light seemed to blossom in his head, followed by an incredible darkness. One brief kneading sensation in his brain, and he lost consciousness.

CHAPTER VI: THE BLUE MUTANTS

Murno was trussed so he could hardly wriggle. He was being carried over someone's shoulder with maddening ease, in such a way that his nose bumped against a smooth back. The skin—light blue—was as even-textured as a young woman's, but not as soft.

He groaned a couple of curses, and from somewhere ahead Gaje's voice called, "Dad! Is that you?"

"Who then?" Murno said sourly. "Where's your mother?"

"She's being carried too, but she's not awake yet."

Murno twisted his head; saw nothing but pine trunks and a spattering of golden sun on a floor of pine needles. "You! Do you speak English?"

A voice—somewhere ahead of his bearer—began to sing. It was an easy croon this time, not discordant, with unexpected shifts of key that were surprising but pleasant. There was no twinging of his muscles—instead, they relaxed. He began to feel drowsy. Suddenly, he struggled and shouted, "Fight it!"

Gaje's voice said sleepily, "I . . . can't . . ."

A moment later, Murno couldn't either. He stayed awake, but in a comfortable lassitude. There was something he should be worrying about, but he couldn't remember what.

The day drifted by. Toward evening, his captors began another chant. This one put him quickly to sleep.

He stretched and rolled over, blinking away sleep, then, remembering, sat up abruptly. He was in a shallow cave floored with soft fragrant green pine boughs. Klayr lay asleep beside him, and beyond her, Sis. The two boys were over at one side of the cave, both beginning to stir.

His hand went to his belt; discovered that his knife and the Gaddyl weapon were gone. He got swiftly to his feet, took four quick steps to the wide mouth of the cave, blinked for a moment in sunshine, then glared at the five beings seated cross-legged in a little arc before the cave.

They were nude except for breechclouts, knife-belts, and moccasins. Their blue skins were all of one shade, and as smooth as Klayr's except for a few faint scars. Their faces were boyishly handsome, their expressions wooden except that he could see, variously, mischief, curiosity, and latent violence in their eyes. They were alike enough to be quintuplets. Their scalps were shaved and shiny blue, except for a small patch of short-cropped blue hair above each one's forehead. The "whites" of their eyes were pale blue; the irises a little less pale. Their ears were—shockingly—pointed on top with tufts of blue hair. They were all lithe and well-formed, but in no way showed the strength Murno knew them to have.

He hesitated, wondering whether he dared demand answers. He restrained his anger. "Why did you seize us? We only want to pass through to the higher mountains!"

Their expressions didn't change.

"Don't you understand English?"

They regarded him gravely for a moment. Then one—the middle one—suddenly opened his mouth and sang one high clear note. After that, they were silent again. But he thought there was more of the mischief in their eyes, now, than anything else.

With a muttered curse, he turned and walked back into the cave. Klayr, Sis, and the boys were sitting up, staring. "They're guards, obviously. Unless I'm wrong, their boss will be along in a minute."

It wasn't much more than that. A blue man strode into sight, carrying two large baskets woven of willow. He was obviously more mature, more bulkily muscled, his skin a little rougher, more scarred, slightly darker blue. His ears were longer and more heavily tufted. He had a full head of hair, cut to about an inch, solidly blue; a small moustache and a little patch of beard, cut short, on the point of his square but rather narrow chin. Like the youths', his cheekbones were prominent, his forehead high, his cheeks slightly concave.

He came casually in and set the baskets just inside the mouth of the cave. "Some roasted corn and yams, and some fresh-cooked venison, plus your own boiled eggs and pork. There's water just along the cliff. We've been told to detain you, but treat you well." His accent was very slight.

Murno stared for a minute. "Uh—thank you. Who wants you to detain us?"

The blue man's broad smile was sudden. "Not the Gaddyl, certainly! Our own patriarch—The Old One. He will be here in ten days, perhaps less. What is your name, and why did you come here?"

Murno fought confusion. Were these blue people savages, or not? "My name's Murno. I'm an em—a Freed Man—from near the bay. It's no longer safe where we lived. I was also drawn into affairs I did not choose; burdened with a responsibility to. . . ." He decided he'd better not talk about that yet. "We were hunted, and I had no choice but to come this way."

The blue man smiled. "You planned well, especially in the matter of the pig-scent."

Murno's mind raced. "Then . . . it was you on the island! And you who drove away the jeel on the other side of the river!"

The mutant looked startled. "There were none of us on the island. But we did divert the first jeel. We kept track of you when you camped, but when you moved suddenly we weren't able to follow at once because of the Gaddyl. Then the pig-scent fooled us for a while—especially since many predators followed it in the night. We only located you again when you used the Gaddyl weapon. That was indiscreet."

Murno said, "I had no choice!"

"No. But it has made problems for us, as well as you. That's one reason The Old One wants to discuss your objectives, and consider whether we can let you reach them. He says you are trying to take something to the Sierra Norms."

"This Old One," Murno growled, "seems to know a lot!"

The blue man smiled his sudden smile. "More than I do, certainly. You are not safe here; we must take you to another place to wait. It would be foolish and useless for you to resist. Can we agree?"

Murno said, "I don't see what choice I have."

"Fine, then. My name is Kah Let. The five outside are my nephews. The leader, the one in the middle, is Liss; the others are his cousins. They will go with you tonight. The rest of the day is yours." He turned and left. The five youths were on their feet in one quick stir, to follow him.

There were, indeed, a spring and a pool a little way along the cliff, offering the chance to bathe and wash clothes. Murno didn't try to scout far. The cave, the pool, and the clearing around them formed a sort of natural unit, surrounded by thick growth. It was beautiful green country, but obviously wild, and he had no idea what might lurk in it besides the blue men.

Just before sundown Liss and his four cousins arrived and stood in a line, waiting silently. Murno entered the cave and picked up his backpack. "I guess we'd better go."

He got a shock. Liss began one of the little chants, Murno, suddenly angry, took a step forward; checked himself; pressed his palms over his ears, hard. "Don't listen to it!"

His action was the cue for five sudden grins. Liss and the others began making odd little gestures, flexing their wrists and clenching and unclenching fingers, turning the hands over, making sudden darting motions or pointing fingers abruptly. Murno felt the familiar drowsiness. He squeezed his eyes shut. "Damn you!"

But it made no difference. Without seeing or hearing the blue men, he was nevertheless asleep within seconds. He realized, as he drowsed off, that his hosts didn't want him to know where he was taken.

The narrow valley had steep and high walls. The floor was no more than fifty yards wide, with a stream twisting down it, and with as much area grown over by flowering shrubs as by grass. It was good to be in green country

37

again. An unfamiliar bird was yammering somewhere, but the squirrels were the ordinary gray kind, scuttling up and down treetrunks.

The young blue men had chopped poles before they left, with which he presumed he was to build a tree-platform. He gave that project to the boys; told them also to help Klayr build whatever kind of cooking-place she thought prudent. He picked up his bow, which the blue men had returned along with his knife and arrows. "I'm going to explore around a little."

He headed up-valley, since the blue men had made gestures that he wasn't to go past a turn a couple hundred yards in the other direction. The sun was warm, but the air was crisp and a little thin——telling him, at least, that the valley was high in the mountains.

The animal signs weren't worrisome——deer, cougar, bear——those wouldn't bother humans unless provoked. A mile above camp, where the valley rose sharply to a higher, rockier level, he found some tracks that evidently belonged to some kind of goat. Later, he encountered an old porcupine stamping grumpily along. Also, he smelled skunk.

Evidently, at some time the valley had been farmed, for there were onions, gone wild; a kind of squash; a small shrub with a sagelike smell, no doubt a seasoning; an some scrawny bean-plants, not doing well. Everything was scattered, though, and if there'd ever been a cottage it was long gone.

He pulled a few of the onions and picked some of the sagelike stuff. On the way back to camp, he thought, he'd knock down a few squirrels so Klayr could make a stew. He needed bow practice, anyway.

He got two squirrels casually, within the first hundred yards, and was getting ready to try for another, higher in a tree, when it suddenly scuttled around the trunk as if it had seen him. He stood there annoyed for a second—was his stalking getting that bad?—before it occurred to him the squirrel might have seen something behind him. He turned quickly.

The five young blue men stood there, in an irregular group this time. They had weapons of some sort—dart throwers, he saw; there were quivers of short darts. He

38

waited uncomfortably for them to make some sound or sign. The look in their eyes was hard to interpret. After a minute, annoyed, he decided to try ignoring them. He turned and began stalking the squirrel.

The little creature was watchful, but it didn't see him move in. It was about thirty feet up the tree, and he was forty or so from the base—not a hard shot. The difficulty lay in anticipating a squirrel's quick dodge. He got the light arrow nocked and drawn.

Something flashed over his head and missed the squirrel by an inch as it dodged. Murno turned. The five mutants were right behind him again! How the devil did they do it? Was he getting deaf?

The one with the dart-thrower in his hand was looking chagrined; the other four derisive. The chagrined one scowled and reached for another dart, at the same instant moving lithely and silently into cover. He was obviously determined to get that squirrel.

So, Murno thought with malice, they wanted to play games? He moved after the young hunter, conscious of his own less graceful gait. He circled, trying to lose himself in the spotty undergrowth.

Trying to stalk that young blue was like trying to stalk a cat at night. When Murno eventually found him, he showed by a casual glance that he knew exactly where Murno was. Murno's ire grew.

But there was still the matter of the squirrel. It had moved higher, and was clinging to the bark with its body at a forty-five degree angle, head lowest, ready to move. Murno studied it while he nocked his arrow. It could dart in any direction, even upward; but he thought it would move horizontally around the tree toward a certain limb.

The young mutant flipped his dart with such an easy quick motion of the wrist that Murno wasn't really ready. His reflexes were, though. His arrow flashed while the dart was still in the air.

As before, the squirrel evaded the dart. But the arrow took it in the back, near the tail. It squeaked once and fell; hit the ground and lay kicking. Murno—suddenly full of shame—hurried forward and killed the suffering thing quickly with his knife. Slowly, he picked up the small body. In a surge of revulsion, he flung it violently into the brush.

Shooting food was one thing. Killing for sport—even grim sport—and not killing quickly and cleanly, was another.

Without surprise, he found the other four blue men once more directly behind him. But now there was approval, even admiration, in their eyes. Perhaps they'd never seen a real bowman before.

They let him go, and he saw no more of them on the way to the new camp. When he was within a hundred yards of that, he began to feel that something was wrong. He crouched listening for a moment, then broke into a run.

The tree platform was finished—and there were braces of freshly-hewed pine, more sophisticated than he would have expected of the boys. And the lashings—those weren't any rope of his!

He stared around. There was a neat circle of round white stones that had never come from this valley; a far tidier fire-spot than needed. Two freshly-cut forked sticks were thrust into the ground on opposite sides, forks up, and several neatly-trimmed pine wands lay handy—cooking-spits. A spot of color at the edge of a trunk caught his eye. He stepped around the tree; found a pair of wild turkeys hanging there.

But where were his people?

He ran suddenly, snarling with anger, to the knotted rope that hung, as a ladder, from the platform; went up furiously. They were all there, on comfortable bough-and-deerskin beds, utterly asleep. He stood for a moment, shaking with anger. Those damned young blue idiots! Murno made a move toward the rope. He found his quivers hanging from new pegs on the treetrunk and grabbed the one that held heavy arrows. He slid to the ground. He took a few running steps up-valley, then stopped. How could he find woodsmen like those?

A clear high note sounded from down-valley: "Mur-no!"

He delayed a moment, caution struggling with rage, then started down-valley at a trot.

He had enough sense to pause after a while and catch his breath while he listened and scanned the pine-covered slopes on either side. He thought the call had come from the shady western side. Slowly, he moved toward it. As he went, a sense of some specific danger grew in him, but he was past caring——until, just among the trees, the feeling suddenly included certainty and direction. He jerked his head around and leaped for a tree-limb and hauled himself up. Murno escaped greedy claws by inches. The feline fell back and bunched itself for another leap, but Murno was already clambering to a higher branch. He stood on that, one arm around the trunk, staring down at the animal. It stared back at him with the expressionless fixity of a cat.

A second one padded silently into sight and sat down near the first, staring up just as intently.

They were no sort of feline Murno had ever seen— perhaps they were some mutation the Gaddyl had made some time, some place. The body-shape was more like a leopard's than a cougar's. But the beasts were big—almost the size of lions though a little of it had to be discounted, as their fur was fluffy. It was splendid fur—almost white, with a few spots of light gray on the backs. The tails, light gray, were long and fuzzy. Just now they lay half-curled about their owners, twitching a little at the ends. These, he knew suddenly, were the beasts he'd half-glimpsed when he and the family were first captured. He noted, now, that they had, indeed, no detectable smell.

He wasn't surprised when the five young mutants strolled into sight and stood watching. He glared down at them for a minute. "You'd better call off your cats if you don't want them full of arrows."

As usual, they didn't respond. After a minute, the one who'd missed the squirrel—Murno could see, now, that he was a trifle more mature than the others—reached for his dart-thower. Murno tensed. The dart came so quickly he had only time to duck his head. When the hardwood dart thunked into the bark above him, he realized the blue man had aimed deliberately high—but not by much. Cheeks burning, he set himself, resolved not to duck the next dart. But the blue man was making gestures—patting himself on the scalp, then indicating by measurements in the air that each successive dart would be lower.

So that was the game. They'd drive him down within reach of the cats. He tensed to reach for his bow——better to die trying to fight back, if it came to that——then he remembered that some patriarch of these strange people

41

had allegedly ordered them to treat him well.

Could he rely on that? Sickly, he thought of his family, marooned here, if he died. On the other hand, how humiliating if these striplings were only bluffing!

He drew in his breath, stood straight up, relaxed, and glared at them. The one with the dart-thrower in his hand——it must be Liss——paused uncertainly. The five of them exchanged glances. Then, in unison, they grinned and began to make familiar weird little gestures with their hands. Murno, suddenly terrified, squeezed his eyes shut. But the kneading in his brain began. He clamped his teeth on a groan; a tiny bit of it forced its way out anyhow . . .

He was falling—falling from a long way, sprawled out and tumbling end over end, clutching at air. Far below, a horde of huge pale felines milled about and reared, staring up at him, ravening mouths agape, claws stretched and straining as if they couldn't wait. The mass of bodies seemed to explode outward, so great was his speed. He struck stunningly; was swarmed over; felt the weight and the heat of the great bodies, the awful claws stripping flesh from his body. His scream shrilled in his ears . . .

And he was clinging limply, drenched with sweat, to the pine trunk. The blue men were watching him gleefully. The two cats were on all fours, crouched, staring up in surprise.

Slowly, the terror drained out of him. Shame, and a cold anger, replaced it. He pretended to shift his footing as if still terrified of falling—but, hidden by the pine-trunk, his right hand stole to his knife, eased it from the scabbard, turned it so he gripped the point, ready to throw. When his arm flashed up and back, he was on balance.

An instant before his quick movement, the blue men went tense, faces startled. Then they leaped for cover. But his first arm-motion was a feint—he wanted them moving, committed. The knife flashed through the air, and caught Liss in mid-leap.

Murno, in his anger, hadn't intended a killing wound—no one could throw a knife that fast or that accurately, anyway. But he wanted to hurt his tormentor. As it was, the slash was more glancing than he had in mind. It sliced across the right buttock. But the blue man's startled,

"Huy!" was a tremendous satisfaction.

Very odd, though, was the expression on Liss's blue face in the instant that Murno was throwing. Clearly, he thought Murno was throwing to kill. But he looked neither frightened nor enraged. He looked, rather, *hurt*—as if a favorite toy had suddenly exploded in his hands, maiming him. And that hurt expression lingered in Murno's mind.

The blues didn't show themselves for five minutes. Then Liss, not limping badly and hardly bleeding, stepped hesitantly from behind a tree. He looked humiliated, but not particularly angry. The other four appeared, grinning broadly. Liss flushed—a purpling of the face—then, suddenly, he laughed. For a full minute he laughed, easily, heartily, then got control of himself long enough to sing a high note at the cats, which immediately trotted toward him. One sniffed curiously at the minor wound, then seemed to ignore it.

Liss called to Murno, "Come on down, Freed Man; the cats won't hurt you now. I'm sorry I gamed with you, but I was angry about the squirrel." He hesitated, then said reluctantly, "You are the best bowman I have ever seen, and I doubt that any of us could match you with the knife either."

"So," Murno said after a minute, "you can talk after all."

Liss looked guilty, then brightened. "The Vow Of Silence may be suspended in necessity. And it is necessary for you to meet the cats, since they will be on guard at the mouth of this canyon. Come on down."

Murno, not comfortably, complied. The cats tensed at first. And then, as Liss crooned a note or two, they relaxed. Soon they were purring and rubbing against Murno as if they'd been his pets all their lives.

Shortly, the blue men and their felines departed. Murno watched them go. Then he turned and hurried to the tree-platform.

The family knew, of course, that the blue men had appeared and put them to sleep, but that was all. They were as astounded as Murno at the camp the mutants had built. Murno decided not to worry his family by telling them the whole of his encounters.

43

For the next five days, they were alone in the valley—though he didn't test the mutants' word by going down to the mouth to look for the cats. The cats might not remember the introduction. He did climb each slope, and saw only rugged green-clad mountains in all directions. He couldn't guess how far he'd been brought, or how near he might be to the Sierra Norms. Certainly, the terrain didn't invite blind wandering.

On the sixth morning, early, he looked over the edge of the platform and saw the two felines sprawled lazily on the ground as if they lived there. His exclamation brought Klayr awake. She sat up with a worried look. "What is it?"

"Some tame felines," he sighed, "that I met the other day. I didn't want to worry you, so I didn't mention it. I imagine we'll have company today." He called down to the cats. One lifted its head briefly, glanced at him with neither surprise nor any other emotion, blinked once, slowly, then put its head on the ground again.

It was half an hour later that the five young blue men walked casually down the western slope. Liss—easily recognizable by his slight limp—carried two fresh-killed wild turkeys. Something looked different about them—Murno realized, finally, that the small patches of hair were shaved off their heads. Liss saw his glance and grinned sheepishly. "Our gaming cost us, Freed Man." He glanced at Klayr, and made a stiff little half-bow. "A pleasant day to your family."

There was, of course, nothing to do but ask the blue men to share breakfast. Only Liss talked during the meal, and he sparingly. Afterward, though, he had business. "The Old One will be in our region soon, and a feast is planned. Much meat is needed, and it would be preferable if some of it were beef. We have come to ask you to hunt with us."

Murno, surprised, faltered, "I don't know if . . ."

Instantly, the blue men all went rigid. Slowly, Liss said, "It is a great compliment we pay you, Normal!"

Murno felt himself flush. "I understand the compliment. But I am not a carefree youth like you. I have my family to look after."

For a moment they stared at him as if they didn't understand; then they looked at each other with odd expressions. Finally Liss chuckled. "I was careless not to

44

mention that your family will be looked after. They will have to move, in any case, so why do you not hunt with us meanwhile? Unless we are too young for you!"

Murno didn't dare hesitate any longer. "In that case, I will be honored to hunt with you."

The mouth of the valley was a narrow rocky gorge which emptied into a wider, lower valley boasting a respectable stream. For most of the day, they descended that.

An hour before sunset, Liss said, "Freed Man, if you will provide a fire we will get fish. It's best we have the cooking done before dark."

Murno had been worried that they seemed to be headed for the Sack Toe Valley. "The Fief who is after me will not give up easily. I'm surprised we've seen no geehawks yet."

Liss looked at him in surprise. "Didn't you know the search had been diverted? Do you think we want breloons among our hills? A few of us crossed the San Wah Keen again, and left false trails leading southwest. Our scent is human. And we dropped a garment of your daughter's—has she not missed it?—and two arrows from your son's quiver."

"Oh." A thought struck Murno. "Can you control Gaddyl as you do—uh, other beings?"

"No. Their minds are too alien. Breloons we can sway sometimes, and geehawks. And the jeel, though alien, are not too hard. But we cannot even touch a Gaddyl mind. The Old One says it is a blessing—else they'd have discovered our talent long ago, and exterminated us."

Murno went about building the fire. He noted that his companions didn't charm the fish out of the water—they drove them into shallows and caught them by hand, as he would he would have, lacking hooks or a net. Later, he asked them about it, and earned incredulous looks. "How naive you are, Freed Man," Liss said finally. "Such a small mind as a fish's . . . one might as well try to control a stone! In any case, we would not use our talents to catch food! That would be as unmanly as taking it away from a child!"

Murno let it go at that.

They entered the Sack Toe Valley far south of where he'd left it. The land was even drier and barer, though

45

the river they followed was adequately screened. Liss explained that there were small herds of bovine here, not much hunted by the Gaddyl, who seldom visited this part of the valley.

After an hour, though, the young blue men began to act odd. Finally Liss told Murno, "You'd best take to cover. There's a feel of geehawks."

Murno scooted for the thicket, and the two felines came with him. The blue men, still in the open, walked slowly so he could keep pace. After a while he called out, "Aren't you worried about being seen?"

"No," Liss said. "We've never dodged Gaddyl. Would it not look suspicious if we did now?"

Murno told him, "You may find it different now." He hustled along, trying to stay hidden and still keep up.

After a while he saw a geehawk diving—then several more. The blue men walked on calmly. The birds circled for a few minutes, screeching uncertainly, then flapped away. Murno hurried close enough to whisper. "Listen— those birds wear radios, and in a minute an aircar will be here to investigate!"

Liss said, "We know that, Freed Man." Nevertheless, he looked worried. Finally he glanced at his cousins, and they all took to the cover. "This has always been considered our hunting territory. But with you along, obviously it is different!"

Murno, beginning to fume inwardly at this foolhardy trip, tried to hurry them along. But they wouldn't listen to him until, somewhere behind them, a clamor of breloons began.

CHAPTER VII: THE GAME OF AMBUSH

The blue men glared back toward the breloon-clamor. The two felines crouched, snarling. Finally Liss, blue face suffused with anger, said, "So they would hunt us?" He glanced around swiftly and moved toward the water. "Come!"

The cats swam as easily as anyone. On the far bank, Liss hustled Murno upstream a ways, then out through the thicket. He chose a big elm at the edge and held his hands to give Murno a boost up. "Hide well, where you can see out over the grass. And have your bow ready!"

Back at the river, the others were doing something— constructing trail puzzles, no doubt. He heard the cats snarl and push through brush somewhere near him, then they were silent—hidden, perhaps. It was some comfort to know they were near. Then he heard the blue men plunge into the river again, and swim back across. What gall!

Now there was only the sound of the breloons. They coursed along the opposite bank, halted, vociferating, where the trails turned toward the water; then quieted to a low grumbling. Aircars, obviously, had landed near them.

Murno perched uncomfortably in the fork he'd chosen. What were the young fools about? Had they decided to abandon him here, and flee home? With their talents, they might evade the pursuit. The cats might be gone, too—he'd only presumed they were still here. Maybe, for all he knew, Liss had arranged things so he'd be discovered after a while—which would give them quite a lead and might, in some twisted thinking, mollify the Gaddyl. Liss—for all Murno knew—might, despite the protestations, hate him. If all that were true, what was Murno's best chance? He didn't know where his family might be now; anyway, he could hardly go looking for them, with Gaddyl close on his trail again. Fool! Why hadn't he just refused this insane trip, and let the young jackasses *be* insulted?

But he did not know what was in Liss's mind; he had no evidence of betrayal. Suppose Liss were depending on him? He'd told him to have his bow ready.

Fool or not, he had to assume—for the time—that Liss would be back.

After a while the breloons began a scattered search along the opposite bank, as if their handlers, before leaving the spot, wanted to pinpoint every trail. Then there was some shouting and disorganized breloon-gibbering—Murno guessed the beasts were being loaded aboard aircars, to be transported somewhere. Across the stream, to this very spot? Would they follow his trail to this tree; clamor around it? Would they flush out the cats? He waited, tense to sickness.

But, instead, the sounds vanished. There was nothing,

for a while, except the gradual resumption by the small creatures of this thicket of their ordinary activities. The breloons could not be near.

Then he heard them again, far upstream and he understood the handler's thinking. Why spend hours combing out trail puzzles? The quarry—whatever it was— would most likely try to double back and get to the hills. The breloons were now set down far enough upstream to intercept such an effort. They'd sweep down on both sides, aided by hawks and aircars, and push the quarry out into the valley.

Which still didn't tell him what Liss intended. Slowly, perspiring, with the familiar leaden feeling in his stomach, he chose arrows and arranged them in his left hand, with the bow-grip. He tested the string and shifted about until he had a passable window to the open. The breloons were getting close now—and they sounded as if they were on a fresh trail. Also, they all seemed to be on this side of the river—maybe the other bunch had already been ferried across to join the new chase.

The clamor suddenly took on a sighting-note. Moments later, the blue men came into sight, running awkwardly as if exhausted. They paused, darting frantic looks around; made little movements toward the trees. Acting afraid of the thicket. A pair of geehawks swooped. The blue men fended them off desperately.

Murno shook with anger. So this was a new game! The mutants were putting on an act—he knew them well enough by now to see that. And he'd been cast in a deadly role—hero or villain, depending on the point of view—but deadly!

Twelve breloons poured into sight and surrounded the blue men. The latter grabbed for knives and formed a defensive ring, acting bewildered and hopeless. An aircar settled from above. There were three Gaddyl in it—a guide, piloting, and two guests, each with a rifle.

Murno steeled himself for the drama he could not avoid.

The aircar was one of the kind used to transport breloons in small packs—four-seated, with a screened-off pen behind. It hovered while the pilot made his little spiel about the blue men. For a moment, he and the guests sat grinning down.

Liss cried out angrily, "Call off your mongrels! We are no slaves, to be harried like this!"

The guide's grin widened. "Things have changed, freak. There is a new Fief, and new rules. You are fair game now. Run a ways, and make better sport of yourselves. Then we shall see whether breloons will eat your flesh or scorn it!"

Liss's motion was so fast it blurred. His knife dropped to the ground. One hand came up with his dart-thrower, the other with a dart. The wrist flickered. The dart flew. A breloon shrieked and toppled, biting at himself. The other beasts leaped in, bellowing. Liss sang out a high note.

The three aliens, grimaces frozen on their faces, were an instant in reacting. Then one rifle jerked up.

Murno's arrow flashed in the sun and took that alien in the middle-chest, below the ribs, where the Gaddyl heart was. Somewhere, the cats roared and charged from hiding. Murno was drawing the other arrow; his target, the guide, was reaching frantically for some weapon. Murno beat him to the shot. But the third Gaddyl's rifle was coming to bear on Murno more deliberately, with no jerkiness, no panic. In the split second that the race lasted, Murno felt a flash of admiration for the alien sportsman—in this sudden surprise, with a deafening melee of felines, blue men, and breloons going on below, with his two companions already dead or dying, he did not falter: he showed no sign of what must roil inside him.

The foliage saved Murno. The alien had to pause just an instant, squinting to see, and Murno's arrow took him.

Murno shouted to Liss, but the aircar was already rising, slanting up and south. Murno grabbed for more arrows, in case they were needed—but the breloons that weren't already dead or crippled were scattering, fleeing for the trees. He heard one scrambling up somewhere near him.

Hurriedly, he slid down from the tree and ran to the blue men. "Are any of you hurt?"

Liss shrugged. "A few scratches. The one you gave me is still the worst." He grinned easily. "What will happen now? Can the Gaddyl find this spot at once?"

Murno stared after the still-rising aircar. "I don't know.

It depends whether the pilot got the transmitter turned on before I killed him. If not, they'll have trouble tracing it, unless they find it right away. It'll climb a few thousand feet, then level off automatically. In an hour or so, some monitor will notice on radar that it's moving steadily south, and try to call it." He scanned the sky. "What became of the geehawks?"

"We sent them home. How about the breloons?"

"They'll go wild, unless they're picked up."

Liss asked calmly, "Have we two hours?"

"Maybe. If not, we'll know within fifteen minutes!"

Liss, gesturing to his cousins, bent to pick up a bloody dart. "We can clean up all the signs, then. And we're not going home without beef. There'll be no other chance to get it for a while."

Murno stared at them incredulously, but he saw no sense in arguing—that would only waste more time. He helped them police the spot. Half an hour later, tight-lipped, he helped them stalk a small group of bovines, and put an arrow into a plump heifer. For the first time, he saw the darts thrown full-arm, and was impressed.

It was dusk before the young cow was butchered, and the offal dumped into the stream. By that time, the cats were gorged enough to be persuaded from their feast. The trek up-river began openly, now, since there were so many fresh trails anyway. Later, they'd wade.

Murno plodded under a burden of meat he wouldn't have chosen without the unnatural competition of the blue men to shame him. He saw that they were subdued, almost sullen. Were they realizing what fools they'd been? Finally, Liss met his glance. "The Old One knows something has happened that will cause trouble with the aliens. We can feel his anger."

Murno, by now, was ready to believe that. He had his own worries. In that runaway aircar, lodged in the corpses, were three of his arrows—recognizable, to someone who knew him well enough.

CHAPTER VIII: FEALTY, THOUGH
ALL ELSE TOTTER

Oory, Chief-At-Arms to the new Fief, Guddun, finished his hasty dip-and-shower and hurried to the closet for fresh garments—a pair of off-duty trousers and a jacket bearing his stripes of rank and the simple sea-and-setting-sun pictogram of Fiefdom Bay. This hurried midnight call demanded no formal dress. Thrusting his splayed feet into wide flat boots, he wiggled his webbed toes until they felt comfortable. He went to the night-stand beside the bed to get the handgun from the drawer. He paused for a moment, looking at the photo of dead Kokiel he still defiantly kept, drew in air between his teeth and lowered his head in obeisance. "Forgive me my thoughts, Friend and Master. He is your son, and I will serve him as I served you."

He holstered the handgun, threw on a loose cape, and strode to the door.

Several of the Staff were in the garage before him— Dobreez, First Mechanic; Emshle, Chief of Communications; Atri, his own nephew and Armory-keeper; Elder Patron Oj Liave. All lowered their heads respectfully as he entered. He made the horizontal hand-sweep that wiped away protocol.

Emshle was just re-casing a small camera. "I have photographed from every angle, Eminence. May we now remove the bodies?"

"One moment." Oory stepped to the aircar that rested under the harsh overhead light. He studied the way the corpses slumped, where the rifles lay, glanced at the instrument settings on the car's control panel. Nictating membranes slid over his eyes momentarily at the cruel way the bodies were transfixed by arrows. He glanced up. "Who piloted the car home?"

Dobreez said, "I did, Eminence. We had no hint of violence—we expected only that an empty car had lifted accidentally. I wanted to be sure if there was a malfunction, so I went myself. We did have to move one body aside, but he's replaced in the same position."

"I hope so," Oory said testily. He bent to peer at one of

the arrows, and the sickness around his heart worsened. A local em's shaft . . . Murno's!

Guddun chose that moment to enter. Oory bowed with the rest. The young Fief, shaking with rage, stood a moment staring at the bodies, his neck stretched high and weaving back and forth. "So!" he exploded finally, "while my servants dawdle, my guests are butchered! Do any of the murdering savages live? I want to watch them roasting!"

There was a shrinking silence. Oory—as senior—steeled himself to reply. "They have not been found, Master. The spot of the tragedy is not yet fixed."

For a moment it looked as if Guddun might reach for his handgun. But words came instead. "Not fixed? Dunghead! What do you mean? For what do I have a Staff? You, Emshle—whence came the first call for help? Why were not rescue cars there at once?"

Emshle's nictating membranes fluttered across his eyes. "There was no call, Master. The car was observed by radar to be——"

"Bowels of Hell!" Guddun searched about for something to destroy; seized an instrument of some sort and shattered it on the floor. "Are you asking me to believe that a party can be ambushed, their car set adrift, a flock of gee-hawks sent home, and a full dozen breloons swallowed up ——and you have no idea where? Stupidity? I vow not! No gaggle of fat-bottomed bed-habiting retainers could be *that* stupid! It is deliberate treason! Treason, I swear!" He stood panting and shaking, eye-membranes aflutter. "You, Oory! If you have any qualifications at all for your soft job, get to the bottom of this! I want those murdering savages screaming on roasting-spits before the night is out!" He whirled toward the door. "I'm going to Ingress and seek competent aid!" He slammed out.

Oory stood a minute, mind racing. Then, "Let's adjourn to my quarters. There's something here that must be aired!"

Oory squatted morosely on a floor-pad, marshalling his words. Let the Staff's uneasiness ferment a moment! Finally he said, "Bay Fiefdom's reputation for pleasant personnel relationships is as old as her fame for providing accomodations and sport for guests. That reputation was not nurtured in secretiveness and intrigues. In moments of trouble, the Staff has been a unit." He let that sink in. Few of them met his eyes. "I do not hint that we should in the slightest way be disloyal to our Fief. I do say—and none of you will contest it—that Guddun is immature and foolish, to the point of possible disaster. Until he matures, our loyalty demands that we co-operate, even conspire, to guard him from the results of his errors. I now ask of you—in dead Kokiel's name, I demand—that we affirm this. Does any demur?"

He saw only averted eyes. "It has become clear to me this night that information has been kept from me, and doubtless from others of you. This loss of two guests and a guide is not a thing to transpire without a prelude." He looked suddenly at Oj Liave. "Elder Patron, I wonder if you have something to confide?"

The official responsible for keeping guests happy (and safer than they thought) slumped on his mat, anguish in his features. Finally he made a forlorn gesture. "Only a few of my guides knew. Guddun swore us to utmost secrecy. He has recently made an agreement with certain other Fiefs— I do not know who—by which they direct to him guests who are willing to pay for the privilege of hunting wild humans."

Oory sighed. A few hours before, he would have been incredulous. Now . . . "Please go on, Old Friend."

The white membranes covered Oj Liave's eyes for a moment. "These guests just murdered had been extended the privilege at no extra charge—provided they helped in the search for the surviving one of the three slaves who recently escaped, and for any of the local ems we suspect of helping them. Also, Eminence,—the party from which the slaves escaped had been sold the privilege of hunting Wild Folk. It has been my speculation, and Guddun's, that the slaves fled in anger after overhearing the guests talk when they paused for a night on the bay before going inland to hunt."

Oory tensed with anger. So *this* was what had turned Murno into a killer! He controlled his voice. "I must thank you, Old Friend, for sheltering me from that knowledge. I am sure it did not occur to you that the knowledge might

53

have helped me in the search, or forestalled more tragedy."

Oj Liave's lips drew back in a grimace of hurt. "Would you have had me, then, betray Guddun at the first opportunity? I did not foresee this trouble. In any case, you might look to your own department for information!" The membranes did not cover his eyes in time to mask the quick glance toward Atri.

Slowly, Oory's head swung toward his Armory-keeper. "You reported to me, son of my eldest sister, that a handgun, powered, was stolen when the slaves escaped. Was there more?"

Atri lowered his head almost to the floor. "Much more, Eminence. It has been a mountain upon my shoulders. That party from which the slaves fled had heard of Wild Folk possessing stolen rifles, or crude firearms of their own. They demanded thorough protection." Atri drew a shuddering breath, then plunged on. "At Guddun's orders, I installed a Mark Four Distorter in their aircar. When the car was returned after the escape, the Distorter had been pried off the panel and was gone!"

Oory sat rigid, in utter amazement. Finally he found words. "God of Rainfall, nephew! You let a Distorter leave the Armory without even consulting me? Don't you know Interplanetary Regulations? The Fiefdom could loose its franchise!"

Atri said sullenly, "I know that a Fief is a Fief. Do you want to hear the rest?"

"If you don't mind!"

"Well, there was an artifact—an ancient human one, presumably—picked up somewhere in the field by some guests. I'd locked it away for safekeeping, but Kokiel's last seizure came just then, and it slipped my mind. After the slave escape, I discovered that the thing was gone." He glanced at Oj Liave. "I do not agree with the Elder Patron's speculations about a spur-of-the-moment flight— for one of the escapees was a gunsmith who had access to the place where the artifact was locked."

The implications seeped into Oory. Suddenly he jerked up his right wrist, bringing his communicator near his lips. "Captain of the Guard! Oory speaks!"

"Yes, Eminence!"

"Top emergency! All Normal slaves to be seized at once,

without warning! Search and confinement until further notice! There is a plot of some kind!"

There were astounded noises from the communicator. "Y-yes, Eminence!"

Oory, on his feet, forced himself to stand still for a moment while his mind raced. That handgun discharge reported by monitors had been east of the Sack Toe Valley, in the foothills—while this last ambush—with arrows—had been miles away, west of the San Wah Keen. He darted looks around. "We may have big trouble. I want your pledge: whatever folly Guddun commits or has committed, he is our Fief. And he is Kokiel's son. We guard him from disgrace or harm—whatever we must sacrifice of our own! Honor, rank, life! If we must deceive him for his own safety, we do so as one. Agreed?"

There was a sigh of relief—obviously, recent events had been gnawing at consciences. "Agreed!"

CHAPTER IX: A TRAP IS SET

Oory's aircar—a two-seater with a sealed canopy—whooshed eastward toward a certain point on the Sierra summit. The Sack Toe Valley unscrolled beneath it. Campfires, here and there, goaded his imagination but told him nothing—they could be Gaddyl parties roughing it; Wild Folk (there were always a few in the valley) or, conceivably, some of the fugitives from Bay, unwary of the search. But as long as there were campfires, he mused, the word of the previous day's massacre must not be around.

That massacre disturbed him more than he'd admitted before the Staff. Assuming a sportsman were to die, probably arrows were no worse than claws or fangs; but the involvement of Murno, as civilized a human as you could find, pointed up how serious Guddun's illicit folly had become.

Illicit? Not precisely—there was no law against hunting Wild Folk; simply an agreement between Fiefdoms; extant, according to history, since the Conquest, and based originally upon the treaty of surrender. Men might once have been a party to it. Now, a simple vote of the Council of Fiefs could overturn it.

Earth would be a mess, he thought uneasily, if that happened. Bloodthirsty Gaddyl from a dozen worlds would swarm here—that was a lesson of history. And there was another lesson that some might not understand as well as he, a professional soldier, did—hunting humans, or any other intelligent aborigines on any subjugated world, must degenerate from sport to annihilation. For intelligent races fought back—as races, not as individual animals under the gun.

Take this wooded, gradually-mounting western skirt of the Sierras he was passing over now—nobody knew how many of the Blue Mutants lived there, but there were a lot. Let just a few hunting parties take pot-shots at *them*, and the whole slope would be unsafe. The only way to pacify it would be to incinerate it clear of trees. And there would go your watershed, and the richness of the Sack Toe Valley, and even the clarity of the bay. Muddy flash floods had ruined hunting-grounds on more than one planet.

He sighed wearily. Disturbing as such prospects were, his present concern was more urgent. He had to recapture that Distorter fast.

The first step was to seal it into a limited area.

The Sierra summit was a logical barrier, since the thief seemed to be headed east. Alone, or with a group? Was Murno with him?

It was not widely known, but the Fiefdom had relations with the Sierra Norm leadership. More than one renegade, trying to get beyond the mountains into unfranchised territory, had been intercepted by the high-dwelling tribes.

He glanced at his chronometer. He'd be over the summit by morning; then, with luck, he could handle his business with the Sierra Norm Overchief and start on southeast in time to reach Ingress by dark.

He wondered what Guddun was doing at the planetary capital. He hoped the young fool wouldn't stir up more trouble for himself.

The glare of the morning sun on the snow made Oory shield his eyes. He set the car to hover a thousand feet above the southern tip of the big lake, and tuned his

56

transmitter to the common waveband. The Sierra Norms would be too wary to answer, but they'd be monitoring. He said in English, "Hello. Hello. This is Oory, Chief-At-Arms of Fiefdom Bay. I want to confer with Donnel, or whoever's your Overchief now. I'll land just south of the lake and wait. If he can't meet me there, tell me where to go."

He let the message repeat at intervals, then landed and sat in the sealed car, wishing he had a breather so he could at least throw back the canopy and feel the sun unfiltered. He resigned himself to a wait; he knew they wouldn't show themselves right away.

This time Donnel was more cautious than ever. It wasn't until nearly noon that two bulkily-clad humans emerged from a thick stand of pine and approached the aircar.

Donnel, Oory recognized. The Overchief had a beard, rust-colored and speckled with gray. His eyes were small and dark, deepset and habitually busy, darting from aircar to sky to the trees closing the meadow in. He was tall, and, beneath the fur parka (turned, now, with the brown side out and the white side in, to blend with treetrunks rather than snow) heavy-shouldered and running to fat. If he had hair on his scalp, the fur hat concealed it all. Oory had never seen him without the hat. The trousers—of some heavy woven material—were dark-side out too, and the leather boots didn't carry the white covering Donnel would wear in the snow. Oory wondered why all the caution. Surely, no Gaddyl guest was going to come up here in this thin air.

Donnel carried (in addition to the crude radio he held before his mouth with his left hand) not one of the Sierra Norm airguns, but the Gaddyl rifle Oory had sold him two years ago. The other man—younger, slighter, beardless, but with black sideburns showing beneath his hat and with frankly curious light eyes—had one of the airguns—a four-foot barrel of steel (laboriously drilled, Oory knew, on primitive lathes powered directly by water-wheels, then as laboriously shaved thin), with a bulky air-chamber shaped to serve also as the stock. Those weapons, in Oory's opinion, weren't really enough better than a good bow and arrows to be worth the making. The gun took several seconds to reload, and would only shoot four or five times

57

anyway before the air-chamber had to be pumped full again.

It was amusing, he thought, that they had to talk via radio when they were only ten feet apart. "Good day, Overchief. Has the rifle satisfied you?"

Donnel shrugged. "It has range, and I can fire more times in a hurry. But game far enough away to need such range is usually across a canyon, not worth the hike. And if the first shot doesn't kill, no worthwhile game is going to wait around for the second."

Oory suppressed a grin. He knew quite well that Donnel's main reliance on the rifle was to reinforce his authority. "Well, I brought along a hundred cartridges. And two forty-five volt batteries for your radios." He reached down and lifted into sight one of the packages. "I'll put them out the jettison-lock." He made no move, though, to do that yet.

For an instant, Donnel's greed showed in his eyes, then he masked it. "Batteries? I wish you'd sell us some real power units. Batteries don't last long."

Oory lied, "We can't make the power units to deliver such low voltage. If you can't use the batteries . . ."

The Sierra leader said a trifle hurriedly, "We can use them, if they don't cost us too much. What do you want this time? Furs? Gold? Cinnabar?"

"None of those. I want a service, this time. And if you can perform it, maybe I can get you another rifle or two. Or whatever you need."

"What kind of a service?"

"There's been a slave escape, and some things stolen. A handgun. Also two highly technological instruments—a kind of direction-finder we use in aircars, and an old human artifact that belongs in a museum." Oory hesitated. Best not tell about the massacre—Donnel's price would go up. "We want any slave, or any em from the Fiefdom, who tries to cross the mountains. Especially, we want a man named Murno, about your age and with a full beard darker than yours. Or any other suspicious-looking strangers." He paused. "I hope none of your people would be foolish enough to dicker with renegades. Or try to keep the handgun. It couldn't be fired anyway without our pinpointing it." He wondered whether Donnel swallowed that. Ac-

58

tually, this far away, it might go unnoticed. Or, in an electrical storm or in some deep canyon. . . . Maybe, he thought, he'd better post a monitor over the mountains, just in case.

Donnel said innocently, "We wouldn't buy stolen goods. We'll be on the lookout. If anyone gets past the—" Oory supposed he'd been about to mention the Blue Mutants, and thought better of it. "A handgun's dangerous. What if some of us get hurt taking him?"

Oory thought for a minute. "We'll pay indemnities, of course."

Donnel looked satisfied. Oory fed the first of the small packages into the jettison-lock; noted that Donnel stayed watchful while the younger man stepped forward to pick up the package. Oory studied the underling. Where Donnel showed only wariness and greed, this one had a hint of animosity. Neither did he act particularly devoted to Donnel. Oory said to the Overchief, "I don't think I've met your companion."

Donnel lifted his radio impatiently. "Bruke; mayor of the closest town. When will you be back?"

"In a few days. Will this same spot be okay?"

"Good as any."

CHAPTER X: INGRESS

Oory let the aircar hover for a few minutes, high over Ingress.

The pre-conquest humans, Oory knew, had called the political subdivision "Arizona." This particular point was a little north of the center of that ancient subdivision. It was hard to realize that the mountains had once been dry and largely bare—now, with the climate tailored to suit his own race, there was a plenitude of lakes and streams and only the eroded, stony nature of the ancient mountains kept them from being as lush as the Sierras.

Two rivers converged to form a handsome lake. On a plateau southeast of the lake—with another river just to the south—the world capital, Ingress, lay like a green, blue, and white gem in the late sun. He'd served here in his youth, as a Cadet Armsman, before his selection by young Kokiel of Bay.

Ingress' diameter—that of the Outer Moat—was four miles. There was, to be sure, a periphery-fence a quarter-mile outside that, but the ground between was scourged bare, and the ring of guard-towers in that bare circle was hardly part of the jewel. They wouldn't be there at all, except to satisfy Interplanetary Regulations.

The concentric Inner Moat was two-thirds the diameter of the outer. The ring between was residential area and, since Ingress wasn't populous, mostly park. Hardly a house but had at least one private pool and of course narrow canals laced across from Moat to Moat. Houses, many of them genuine native marble, looked smothered in the ornamental forests. Just now, you couldn't see a lawn that wasn't in shadow, so the over-all effect was dark green.

There were no residences inside the Inner Moat, except Occupation Headquarters barracks; a few small cottages for caretakers, museum curators and such—and the hotels and inns. What hotels and inns! Clustered mostly to the south, of course, around the huge square building of Translocation Center—Earth's only link with the rest of the Gaddyl Empire, unless you wanted to spend twelve years or more on a slower-than-light vessel—but scattered, too, all about the circle. Except at the north. That sector was Occupation Headquarters, with its Command Hall, barracks, hangars, armories, and recreation fields. Oory's throat constricted with memory of his young days there.

There were fewer canals within the Inner Moat; more grass and fewer trees, since off-planet visitors wanted to stroll about. But to the east and west of the midpoint, long lakes, bordered on either side by the museums, reflected the deepening blue of the sky.

Yes, truly, Ingress was a gem. And one of the things that kept it that way was the constant flow of fresh water—pumped through great tunnels from the pure lake to the north, drained away through other tunnels to the southern river. Visitors said that no body of water, on any world, was as pure blue as the lakes and canals of Ingress beneath a clear Earth sky.

He sighed, let the aircar drift down toward the landing-lot at Occupation Headquarters and reached for the transmitter-switch. "Oory, Chief-At-Arms, Fiefdom Bay, calling Occupation."

The reply was prompt and impersonal. "Oory, we have you on radar. Will you want to land at Occupation Headquarters?"

"Yes."

"Very well. Hover at five hundred feet. Do you care to state your business now?"

"I'd like to arrange a meeting with His Primacy, Marshal Stolm, as soon as possible."

There was a shocked pause. Staff officials from outlying Fiefdoms didn't just drop in casually and ask for audiences with the highest military authority on the planet. "Your request will be conveyed."

Oory said with a touch of mischief, "Thank you. Will you do me the favor of routing it through Adjutant Elzewain?"

The voice said, a little testily, "We will, Your Eminence."

Oory reached specified altitude and touched a stud to put the car under monitor control; sat waiting while he was shunted into a traffic pattern two or three layers higher than if he'd been a really important visitor.

After ten minutes the radio tower called him again. This time the voice was surprised and respectful. "Oory—Your Eminence—His Primacy asks that you dine with him. An aide will be waiting when you land."

His Primacy, Marshal Stolm, held out a hand to be shaken in the human style. "I've missed our hunts together, Old Friend! It's been galling here lately—planetary politics, a constant stream of guests with petty complaints you'd think any mere guide could mollify, and always some fool or other of a celebrity from the Home Worlds to be entertained. I swear I'm looking forward to retirement! How are the wife and children?"

"Visiting her father, who's ill. I'm glad they're away right now." Oory waited to see whether Stolm would take the gambit. Stolm didn't. A matter had to be very urgent for Stolm to discuss it before dinner.

The dinner—just the two of them, since Stolm's family was off-planet somewhere on a trip—was simple but

61

superb. A salad of crisp aquatic herbs with a dressing of sour wine, salt, pepper, garlic, and tiny shrimp, beaten into a froth with raw duck-eggs. A great succulent roast of cowbison, seasoned with sage and nutmeg. Pickled vegetables. Baked whole potatoes with sour sauce. Tiny birds' eggs, boiled hard. Dark and light wine—and, to dally with while mutant-human slaves cleared away the ruins of earlier courses, a big platter heaped with small brook trout very simply prepared—their heads snipped off, entrails flushed away through slit bellies, then—tails, fins, and all—deep-fried in butter to a brown crispness. Oory suppressed a belch; he hadn't eaten this way in years. What he'd like now would be a lazy swim in warmed water, then a nap.

But Stolm was ready to talk trouble. "Your new Master was here today. I was going to summon you, if you hadn't come."

Oory made a slight neck-bow to signify he was listening.

"This," Stolm went on, "is a popular resort world, considering the distance. The popularity and the distance guarantee us one thing: the guests we get are nearly all prominent or wealthy, or both. So we must pander to them."

Oory tried to stay alert. He wished he hadn't eaten and drunk so well.

"Those two you lost in the Sack Toe Valley," Stolm said, "were important enough to bring a lot of criticism down on us. I'm going to need a good story."

That, Oory knew, meant really that someone must be a scapegoat. He said nothing.

Stolm said, quietly but suddenly, "How did you lose the Distorter, Oory?"

Oory jerked his head aloft, ready to make an angry denial. He stopped, with his mouth already open. So Guddun had admitted the loss! That took a heavy burden off Oory.

Or did it? Had Guddun blamed *him*?

He opened his mouth again to tell Stolm the truth—and it was as if dead Kokiel spoke somewhere in the back of his mind. He closed his mouth and, slowly, forced himself to relax. "There was confusion in the change-over, Stolm. Guddun was not immediately aware of certain things. I may have assumed responsibilities I should not have, and I may have made mistakes."

Stolm's teeth showed in a grimace that was not quite a smile. "A noble speech. I speak now as a friend, Oory, and in confidence. Someone will have to take the blame. The Distorter is a serious matter; even the miniature version Guddun lost. On this planet, it means nothing—we could hand them out by the dozens to our Wild Folk, and they could find no better use for them than for so many rocks. But High Command at home does not see that, and will not wish to see it. There are subjugated worlds where the natives retain enough technology to seize upon a sample of the Distorter, study it, and in time learn the science of space distortion. There are worlds from which a small Distorter might be smuggled, eventually to reach the hands of races we have never been able to conquer. Also—High Command will note that humans once possessed real weapons of their own, and that but for the Distorter they might have fought us off."

Stolm paused, reached idly for one of the fried brook-trout, glanced at it unseeingly, and put it down. "I know Guddun lied—it was he, not you, who let the Distorter get stolen, and who created the circumstances that led to that massacre. But you know I cannot denounce a Fief. However much they may compete, and even squabble among themselves at times, they would close ranks like herd bulls against mere soldiers like you and me!" He leaned across the low table and placed a hand on Oory's wrist. "There must be a goat, my friend, but it need not be you. Some underling—as you say, there was much confusion following Kokiel's death; we can prepare a story."

Oory felt himself flush. Stolm should know him better than that! "There was another matter I came here to discuss, Your Primacy."

Stolm's nictating membranes slid across his eyes for a moment. "Discuss it, then."

Oory chose his words carefully. "Certain guests have apparently taken advantage of our temporary lapse of firmness. The two who were killed brought the trouble upon themselves by trying to hunt Wild Folk." He hesitated, and decided to leave it at that.

Stolm said, "Guddun gave me a different story. He spoke of a slave escape, and of hostility among some ems. All *your* fault, of course. I prefer a third version: Guddun gave the guests permission to hunt humans. I suppose you will deny that?"

"I deny it," Oory said.

Stolm made a derisive gesture. "All right. If you refuse to help yourself, just what is it you want from me?"

"I want you," Oory told him, "to reaffirm publicly the policy that humans, mutant or normal, are not fair game and are not to be hunted or harassed without provocation."

Stolm grunted; reached for one of the fried fish and swallowed it in one gulp. "I'm sure you know that the policy was not set by Occupation Command."

"But," Oory pressed, "Occupation Command does have authority to enforce it!"

"Only if security's threatened. And that's hardly possible, on Earth."

Oory said in some anger, "You'll admit it would place a strain on your garrison if you had to police the whole planet! There are something like twenty-five million Wild Folk, norms and mutants, in North Am alone. What's your professional army? Five hundred?"

"Six hundred. Plus some patrol-craft pilots and crew. Obviously, I don't want the whole planet in turmoil."

"Well, then, what are you going to do?"

Stolm pounded the floor with a fist—the first real sign that he was inwardly uncalm. "I'm going to think, first of all! I can't afford to do anything irreversible without planning! Then I'll probably sound out several of the Fiefs; see if they can muster enough votes to reaffirm the policy. If Kokiel were still alive . . ." He looked straight at Oory. "I have to cope with situations off-planet as well as on, you see? I'll do what I can. But if I can't do what I'd prefer, I'll do what I must!"

"I understand," Oory said quietly. "In any case, I know what you do will be honorable."

Stolm sighed, the membranes sliding across his eyes, then got to his feet. "One last swim together, while we can still be friends?"

Oory lowered his head solemnly. "One last swim."

CHAPTER XI: THE OLD ONE

It was morning. Murno walked with Kah Let, who'd met the misadventurous party the day after the massacre, while they were still climbing the foothills. Liss and his cousins were up ahead somewhere, hurrying the meat to its destination.

Kah Let had a puzzled air. "I should have thought The Old One would be enraged, but all I feel from him is disgust and . . . I would have to call it resigned concern. You must wish now, Freed Man, that you'd fled in some other direction!"

Murno said listlessly, "There was no other direction I could go. Anyway, with Guddun ruling Bay, there'd have been no peace for my people or for yours. What will you do now? Can you migrate?"

"Hardly; there are too many of us. But The Old One will decide."

They walked in silence for a while. Then Murno began to notice something expectant and perhaps amused in Kah Let's manner. Shortly, they rounded a canyon-shoulder and Murno's eyes lit on a small camp. Moments later, Gaje was running toward him. "Dad! Dad!"

The family's camp was in a corner of a granite cliff, adequately hidden by pines, with a trickle of water nearby. Klayr was tearful with relief. "The mutants who brought us here wouldn't say anything, but I was sure something awful had happened!"

Murno hesitated. "We had a little trouble, but we got clear all right."

Gaje demanded, "Can we go on now and find the Sierra Norms?"

"I don't know yet. I'm going to see a patriarch of some kind today. I'm afraid you'll have to wait here, but you'll be safe and comfortable."

The canyon he and Kah Let climbed was very steep; rocky, with a tumbling stream. They met other blue men along the way—Murno thought all the mature men in the region must be gathering.

They passed a tributary canyon where women and children were camped.

The women were daintier than the men, but all moved with the same animal litheness, and he saw some of them lift burdens that he'd have strained at himself. They wore their dark blue hair in braids or "pony tails." Their garments—light jackets and loose breeches that reached only to mid-thigh—were mostly of deerskin, but he saw hand-woven fabrics too. They wore heelless ankle-high shoes of soft leather, or moccasins, and some of them wore beads or bracelets of bone or carved wood. They were merry and gregarious among themselves, but only the older ones spoke.

The children were slim and pale blue and silent, melting in and out of the forest, but full enough of mischief. Many of the boys had dart-throwers; the girls carried dolls. Their unnatural silence didn't seem to hinder their play.

Women and children, they stopped to stare, without expression, at Murno as he passed. He heard one old woman say to another, "Not a Sierra Norm. Must be from the lowlands!"

The canyon ended in a great cirque, from the rim of which a thin waterfall spilled. The pines grew thick, and beneath them were tables—long things with benches on either side. Murno could smell the feast before he saw it. He paused, a little uncomfortable under the grave regard of the several hundred mature blue men who stood about, apparently not yet privileged to seat themselves; then forced himself to walk on beside Kah Let.

The wonderful smells came from cooking-fires along one edge of the cirque. Spitted above them were haunches of beef; whole small deer, lamb, pork, turkeys and grouse and ducks and geese, squirrels, rabbits, and a dozen other varieties of small game. Banked around the fires on iron racks were great flat loaves of bread, forming their own ovens. Huge iron cauldrons, no doubt holding grains and greens, steamed and bubbled. Young blue men—all of them, Murno noticed, with completely-shaved heads—moved about stirring the pots, turning spits and loaves of bread. He recognized Liss, but the young man wouldn't look at him.

Then all eyes turned to the head of the cirque. Murno

saw The Old One emerge from a cave behind the waterfall. He stared, feeling goose-pimples all over himself.

Age had bleached The Old One's hair, but had not taken it. A blue-tinged silver cascade, it hung down his back to the waist. He was just now binding it into a loose tail, absently, as he stood surveying his assembled tribesmen. He had no beard, no moustache. Maybe, Murno realized suddenly, the Blue Mutants grew no facial hair, except for those ear-tufts. The patriarch's skin was darker than that of his juniors, and it did show age—it was toughened, creased, and hatched with a thousand old scars—but it was certainly not senile. Nothing about him was! The old face was etched and shaped as if by a million smiles, a million frowns, but it was the alert face of a vigorous man. And his body! He wore only the breechclout and weapon-belt and moccasins. If his muscles were not as lithe and young-looking as, say, Kah Let's, they were awesome in their bulk, their hardwood solidity. His proportions were regular and athletic, though he was huge—as near seven feet tall as six. The thought flashed through Murno's mind that here was a patriarch who need not rely on his age to win respect.

As if he guessed Murno's thoughts (and, Murno wondered a little sullenly, could he not?) The Old One smiled at Murno and gestured toward a small table with two individual benches. His voice was surprisingly soft and young. "Will you come sit with me, Freed Man? There are things we must discuss."

The purple wine was strong, and Murno was careful not to drink too much of it. Dizzying enough, to sit across-table from this astounding being, trying to hold up one end of a casual conversation.

A young man brought a full skin of wine, and Murno met his eyes; started. Liss grinned sheepishly and turned away.

The Old One stared after Liss, with an odd expression. "At least, he can carry food without dropping it." He turned to Murno. "I don't believe Kah Let has adequately apologized for the harassment you've suffered. I hope you can forgive the young men." He watched Murno for a moment. "You do not like us much, Freed Man, and I

67

cannot blame you, but you are reasonable. And since your destiny has become braided with ours, I am going to tell you things that no other Normal has known for many generations. First of all, how old would you judge Liss to be?"

Resentment urged Murno's tongue. "Since you can read my mind, why bother to ask?"

The Old One Smiled. "I cannot read your thoughts, except that I can feel your emotions. If they are strong enough, and I happen to be concentrating on you or your immediate surroundings, I can feel them a long way. I felt, for instance, your torment when you were forced to kill the three Gaddyl. I had already become aware of Liss' folly in taking you to hunt with him, and I was concentrating. But I cannot invade your thoughts."

Murno said sullenly, "No? I've been put to sleep, and had my head filled with delusions, and manipulated like a doll. Wouldn't you call that invading my thoughts?"

"Not precisely." The Old One cut himself a slab of meat and put it on a chunk of bread; chewed briefly; swallowed. "If you'll think back, my descendants only manipulated your *feelings* on each occasion. Any detailed thoughts— even the nightmares you may have suffered—arose from your own imagination. One of those nightmares has been described to me. Liss' felines had treed you; your strongest emotion at the time was fear of the cats. Liss and his cousins exploited it. Your own mind supplied the details." He gulped wine. "Believe me, our talent is a long way short of reading abstract thoughts. In any case—perhaps it is too soon afterward to say this to you—you were not harmed and you had a thorough demonstration." He looked idly about for a minute. "My descendants are quiet. They understand the trouble we face." He looked back at Murno. "I'd asked your guess of Liss' age."

Murno said impatiently, "Oh, nineteen or twenty. A couple of years older than his four cousins."

The Old One smiled. "We do not mature as fast as Normals. Liss is one hundred twenty-seven. The other four range from ninety to one hundred eight."

Murno stared at him. The blue being must mean seasons, or something! Then, looking into the seamed old

68

face, a cold doubt began to creep up his spine. In a shaky voice he asked, "And . . . you?"

The patriarch sighed. "I look back upon nearly seven centuries. I feel that I may live another." He watched Murno for a moment. "When the Gaddyl created us, Freed Man, they unlocked from the human genes far more than they intended or dreamt possible. Do you know anything of our history?"

"Why, no . . . just that you've always lived along this slope of the Sierras."

The Old One nodded. "Mostly. The Gaddyl do not know our history now, and in telling it to you I am gambling. You will understand that it gives you a weapon against us but, possessing it, you may hate us less." He got up, walked a few steps, and stared around the hollow for a minute; came back and stood looking down at Murno. "There were two dozen or so in the original experiment brought to puberty. When strange powers began to show, the group was destroyed. All except two males, who escaped. My grandfather was one. His brother—they were all siblings—vanished, and no doubt died in some mishap. My grandfather hid, and lived, and in time mated with various Normal women. I am only half Blue Mutant, Freed Man." He sat down again. "My grandfather, so it is told, died in a fall off a cliff when he was younger than I am now. I have no surviving brothers. I have one surviving son, who is over three hundred, and aging fast. Some of my grandsons are over two hundred fifty, but I do not think any of them will see three hundred. Do you see the significance, Murno?"

Murno, dazed, shook his head. "Unless . . . the normal blood . . ."

The patriarch nodded. "We think that's it. The mutation is receding. It isn't only the longevity—the talents seem to fade with each generation, even though no more Normal blood has been introduced. Liss and his cousins, for instance, have less than Kah Let—who, by the way, is a hundred eighty-odd. If it weren't for the Vow of Silence—if Liss had been allowed to communicate, as a child, by talking—the talent would hardly have developed in him at all." The blue being sat, pensive, for a while. "We didn't find that out until four hundred years ago; that's when we

69

imposed the Vow on our young. We don't know how it's going to work out—we don't know where we're going as a species."

Murno endured silence for a moment, then, "How is it that the Gaddyl have left you alone? Surely they must know—"

"They know nothing. The Fief who had us created later expunged the records, as the experiment was illegal anyway. And, as we were assumed destroyed, no one searched for us. When subsequent generations of Gaddyl encountered us, we gave them a false legend. We've succeeded in avoiding them most of the time. Until now." He stared toward the young men tending the fires. "I and my grandsons have been able to keep things in hand, but now our descendants are getting so numerous . . ." He looked hard at Murno. "This is deadly knowledge you've just gained. Many of us have died to protect it."

Murno, not happy having it, said, "I don't see why you've given it to me."

The Old One got to his feet again, restlessly. "Because we need you. Word has reached us of the new Fief of Bay, and his intentions toward Wild Folk. We must prepare. For one thing, I hope to make peace with the Sierra Norms, and eventually an alliance. I must investigate the possibility of migrating eastward, beyond the mountains. We are not comfortable away from the trees, but there may be wooded places beyond the dry lands—perhaps the Black Grove—where we can exist. And there is another way in which you can be useful to us."

Murno tried not to scowl. "What way?"

"You," the patriarch said, "have been a slave. You know the ways and the capabilities of the Gaddyl. I want to draw upon your knowledge."

Murno sat thinking. Being useful to the blue men, of course, was a sort of insurance. On the other hand . . . "Does that mean that my family and I are prisoners?"

His host took time in answering. "I've been giving that much thought. I'd prefer to have you an ally if I can." He eyed Murno for a moment. "Will you tell me why you want to reach the Sierra Norms?"

Murno squirmed mentally. In his situation, he couldn't

see how to lie successfully. "Partly because I have to get my family out of Guddun's reach, and the Sierra Norms seem like the best chance. Then there's another reason that may have less sense in it." He hesitated. "When I was young, there was a very secret organization among the slaves at Fiefdom Bay. Its purposes, as I look back, were vague, but one of the things we whispered about was the Sierra Norms. They had dreams, we heard, of an uprising some day against the Gaddyl. Not that we believed anything so fantastic as that the Sierra Norms could war against the Gaddyl, but . . ." He looked straight at the blue man for a moment. "Have you ever heard a legend about a being called 'Omha'?"

The Old One Smiled. " 'Omha Abides!' So you were one of those. Murno, you are not the first fugitive to reach us. In my youth, there was more talk of Omha than there is now. The Sierra Norms believed in him then. I can only tell you that nothing substantial has ever reached my ears from the east, except vague talk of a tribe called the Burnies who worship Omha. The legend was one that might easily arise from the bitterness and hope of a newly-conquered people: somewhere, vaguely east of here, an immortal creature, or a tribe of humans, or a spirit of some kind, had gone into hiding to wait the day when an uprising might be possible. I will tell you my own guess: some leader of the ancients did go into hiding, hoping to resume the fight, but died without ever finding the chance."

Murno sat trying to sort out his feelings. "Then the Sierra Norms no longer believe?"

"Their Overchief does not, at any rate—a man named Donnel who is no friend of ours and whom I would not trust. Still . . . those instruments you were carrying. I presume they were smuggled out of the Citadel?"

"Well . . . yes. That's why the search is still on."

The Old One nodded. "I guessed that. Well, whatever technology the race of men still possesses is in the hands of the Sierra Norms; they would be best able to study the Gaddyl science. We blue have foresworn technology, lest it cost us our talents." He drew his knife and sat idly toying with it. "Those instruments must have importance, else the search would not be so intense. Perhaps I had better let you

71

go on to the Norms, Freed Man. But with reservations. We might substitute less valuable items, and observe what Donnel did with them."

Murno said, "I don't understand."

His host used the knife to cut another slab of meat—though the feast seemed to be breaking up for everyone else—and chewed thoughtfully. "From time to time various Gaddyl devices have come into our hands, and I've stored them away without any definite plan. None of them, I think, has much value. Now, suppose Donnel felt it would be profitable to betray anyone coming to him with stolen instruments. Would it not be better to have made a substitution?" He looked at Murno speculatively. "If I merely told you Donnel was not to be trusted, you might doubt my motives. Therefore, I'm inclined to let you test him out for yourself, if you wish. If he plays fair—we'll watch him closely—we can give him the real contraband that you brought all this way. I have a selfish motive in this too, Freed Man. If things work out right, you might become a go-between, to help us make an alliance with the Norms. At the worst, you would be a spy for us."

Murno found the whole thing confusing and tried to puzzle it out. "If you're that doubtful about the Sierra Norms, maybe I can't risk taking my family there."

The Old One grinned broadly. "I am glad you see that. It saves me telling you that I could not in any case let you take them along."

Murno felt himself flush. "I see. Well, I won't pretend to like it. But I guess I haven't much choice. When do I start?"

"Tomorrow." The ancient being reached for his wine took a sip. "There is one other thing I want to ask you about——something you said to Kah Let that puzzles me. You were on some island in the San Wah Keen river, and the behavior of some animal made you think, later, that we'd been influencing it."

"Oh. Yes, a pig. I flushed a bunch from a wallow, and all but one swerved wide of a certain tree. That one blundered close to it, then stopped dead still and stared at it for a moment. I wondered—"

He broke off as the giant blue man came to his feet, kicking back the bench. A big hand reached out and seized

72

his shoulder. "A tree? A *tree? Where is that island?*"

Murno, startled, tried to twist free. "Why—I don't know the country! Kah Let can tell you where it is!" The grip eased. He pulled away and rubbed at his shoulder.

The patriarch took a deep shuddering breath. "Forgive me, Murno. Maybe it means nothing, but . . ." He grinned suddenly, fiercely. "Freed Man, in my long life I have seen that certain men are chosen by Destiny, so that their lives move in strange directed patterns. I do not try to explain it—it is so." He turned and called out down-country in a high clear voice. Then, "Go on your mission to the Sierra Norms, Freed Man. When you have learned what you must learn, return to us. I think you and I will be planning together!"

CHAPTER XII: THE SIERRA NORMS

"Stand where you are, stranger!"

The voice bit at Murno suddenly from his left. He stood motionless, giving them time to size him up, shivering a little in the high thin air.

Presently one of them stepped from behind a pine-trunk ahead. The man was thirty or so, of medium build beneath his bulky parka, the hood of which was thrown back to reveal curly black hair and sideburns. The clean-shaven thin face was heavily tanned. The light-gray eyes were cool and steady.

The Norm carried one of the odd air-rifles. Suspended on a thong around his neck was some instrument, wooden-cased, about the size of a man's moccasin—a clumsy two-way radio, perhaps. One other bit of gear was visible—a monocular field-glass thrust into a pocket of the parka.

The man's lips quirked in a cold smile. "Well? Are you a dummy, like the Bluies who brought you?"

Murno blinked. "Uh . . . no. I'm an em from Fiefdom Bay. I've some instruments I'm supposed to bring you." He hesitated. "Omha Abides!"

There was a chuckle from behind him. The man in front said, "If he does, he doesn't do it here. What's your name and who sent you?"

"I—well, there was a slave escape, and I inherited the job of bringing some contraband to you. My name's Murno."

The man blinked once, but his face didn't change. "Is that so? Well, my name's Bruke. I'll have to hold you for Donnel, the Overchief. Take off your pack and set it down, then stand two paces away from it." As Murno made a half-protesting gesture, the man added, "We don't know what you're carrying. We have to be careful."

Murno shrugged out of the pack and set it down. A second man—older—appeared from behind him, approached the pack, and held an irregular-shaped contraption near it, at various angles. "Doesn't seem to be broadcasting anything." He stepped away.

Bruke nodded to Murno. "Open it, slowly. Take everything out, one item at a time, and lay it on the ground."

Murno, holding his temper, complied. When the contents were laid out, there were ten minutes of careful scrutiny and prodding, then Burke nodded. "Looks all right. Repack it, and let's go."

The shack was evidently the local lock-up. Murno, tired of peering out the single tiny window, lay on the bunk, morosely pondering things.

This was a minor village—there weren't over four families. The other half-dozen shacks seemed to be stop-over spots for hunting parties; he'd seen two buck deer carried in. There was none of the industry here that could drill rifle barrels and build radios, albeit crude ones.

Bruke and the others here didn't seem the least interested in the instruments he'd brought, beyond idle curiosity. The handgun (a useless one, substituted for the good one) made Bruke's eyes sharpen for an instant, until he saw it was exhausted and without a power unit; then he lost interest.

Maybe they had more technology than he realized—maybe they recognized as useless the two battered instruments The Old One had given him. Or maybe The Old One was right about the Sierra Norms.

He rolled over restlessly. Here he was locked up without

his bow or even his knife, and no idea what was going on. He should have listened to the mutants! Or better still, he should never have gotten mixed up in this lunatic mission. He might have fled south in the Sack Toe Valley, avoided the larger waterways and the good hunting country—holed up somewhere until the worst of Guddun's search was over then found a new home for his family far from Fiefdom Bay.

Well, he hadn't. Now he had to hope Donnel would turn out to be all right.

It was past noon. The man who approached the shack with several others on his heels—including Bruke—was big, with a rust-colored beard. His small, deepset dark eyes flickered over Murno. His right hand possessively gripped a Gaddyl sporting rifle, almost as if it were a scepter of office. He grinned in a humorless way. "I hear you came a long way to see me."

Murno said carefully, "I had other reasons. Bay Fiefdom's changed hands, and the new Fief's a harsh one."

Donnel looked blank, then his face twisted for a moment. "New Fief? What's his name?"

"Guddun. Kokiel's son."

"Hm." Donnel's right hand gripped the rifle a little harder. His small eyes narrowed in thought. "No friend of you ems, huh?"

"No friend at all."

Donnel grinned the mirthless grin. "All right. Let's go look at those things you brought."

The items were in another cabin which was apparently a sort of town office. Bruke moved things off the desk to make room for the Gaddyl instruments. Donnel reached greedily for the handgun; turned it quickly butt-up and scowled at the empty power-socket. "Dead!" He looked up narrowly at Murno. "You know what's supposed to go in here?"

"Of course."

"Where'd you get this?"

"A slave escapee brought it to a neighbor. The neighbor sent it to me to bring here."

"Like this? Unpowered?"

75

"Yes."

Donnel swore angrily, and scowled in thought. "Same way with the other things?"

"Yes." Murno wasn't going to talk any more than he had to.

Donnel thrust the handgun into a pocket. He turned sullenly to the other things. "Radar." He searched for and found the fasteners pried the back off and stood looking at the works. "Ordinary battery." He handed the thing to Bruke, who looked resentful for an instant, then picked up the back and replaced it.

Donnel was bending over the other item (which, Murno could have told him, was a water-analyzer), peering at connectors and markings. He straightened, eyes hard, and looked at Murno. "All three of these things are Gaddyl, right?"

The question hit Murno like a mallet-blow. He struggled with his face. One of the things he'd actually smuggled out of Bay was *not* Gaddyl!

Donnel had been expecting him.

Very carefully, he said, "Of course." His mind raced, assessing his situation. Donnel carried the rifle. Bruke had leaned an air-rifle in a corner, but could reach it in one stride. The third Norm in the cabin also had an air rifle, in his hands, and he was watchful. No chance for a break now.

Donnel grinned his humorless grin. "Well, fine, we can use the parts. What were your plans for yourself?"

"Well . . . I have to stay away from the Fiefdom."

"Ha, ha!" The false joviality was sickeningly thick. "Well, we can fit you in somewhere. There's jobs you can work at, or if you can hunt, you can make a living that way. I understand you're friends with the Bluies. We run into them sometimes."

Murno said, "Well, they seemed anxious enough to pass me along. I don't know how they'd act if I met them again."

Donnel shrugged. "Anyway, there's not room for you in this town. Why don't you come back with me to my headquarters?"

Murno feigned willingness. "Why thanks. I want to earn my way, of course."

76

The trail climbed north out of the high shallow valley. As The Old One had described the country, they must be heading toward the south end of the big lake. A couple of scouts moved ahead. Donnel followed them, sometimes turning to talk to Murno. The four who followed weren't obvious about watching Murno, but they were there. He tried to act cheerful and not too bright. Certainly—unless a very good chance offered itself—he wasn't going to try his break right away. He'd have to size them up, give them a chance to grow careless.

What was Donnel's relationship to the Gaddyl? The Old One predicted it would be purely selfish. Someone from Bay, then, had hired the Norm Overchief to intercept fugitives. Why hadn't they killed Murno already? Maybe the Gaddyl specified live captives. Or, maybe, Donnel was just marching him to a rendezvous on his own feet, so he needn't be carried.

It was mid-afternoon now. His captors acted as if they'd be at headquarters before dark. He could not, obviously, wait until then.

He made his decision when he saw they were approaching a deep canyon.

The trail climbed briefly, short-cutting around a ridge. He began to lag and breathe hard. Donnel paused, hiding a scowl. "We won't be climbing much more."

"Thanks . . . I'll make it . . . just not used to this air." Murno plodded on. The trail crossed slanting ground. A few yards below, there was a hump, and from that a sharp drop-off. He pretended to stumble; let himself fall, sliding and clutching. He heard Donnel bellow, "Help him, you fools!" He let himself go over the drop-off, slid ten yards, flailing; half-gained his footing and plunged toward the nearest pine-trunk. Donnel was stumbling and sliding down the milder slope ahead. Murno staggered to the treetrunk, pretended to check himself—then darted around it and went down-slope as fast as he could without losing all control; from tree to tree, checking himself just enough each time, then launching out at an angle. Now Donnel's shout held realization and rage. A bullet tore into bark. The Overchief was screaming at his men to spread out so they could get better shots. Two more bullets whanged by him—but he was gaining on the pursuers, who had to stop to aim.

There were thickets of brush in the bottom of the canyon. His lungs were afire now, but he forced himself to go on, forced his collapsing legs to hold out a little longer; plunged into the brush and fought his way in a few yards, angling a little up-canyon. Then he sat down and let his lungs fight for air.

The shouting upslope stopped, as Donnel realized it was masking any noise Murno might make. He stayed there, motionless, like some completely winded animal. This respite could only last a few minutes at best—they'd see his trail in the brush. But he could do nothing while he was in this condition. He tried to make his breathing as quiet as possible.

There was perhaps twenty yards of brush between him and the stream in the bottom of the canyon. Evidently it wasn't big—he could hear only a murmur, though the bed must be fairly steep. There'd be another thicket on the far slope. If he could get to the creek without being seen or being hit by a blind shot—they'd hear him the instant he moved, of course—he might run along the creek a ways and enter the brush on the other side somewhere.

But all the advantages were with them. They were used to the altitude; younger; could get more help if they needed it. Down-canyon somewhere was Donnel's headquarters. They knew the country up-canyon; he didn't. And he hadn't so much as a knife.

His lungs were easing a little now. He'd have to make his move in the next minute, he felt. Very carefully, he tensed to rise—

There was a sound perhaps fifty yards away, down-stream and across it, as if someone were pushing into the thicket there—trying to get up the opposite slope. He heard Donnel, somewhere above him, snarl an order; heard somebody start down-canyon toward the sound. A rock clattered down to the creek—from the opposite slope—and a human voice that could have been Murno's muttered a curse. Now Donnel and all his men were shoving into the brush, Donnel mouthing obscenities as the quarry seemed to be almost getting away. Murno stayed where he was, listening hard. Was this a trap?

Ten minutes went by. He could tell that the Sierra

78

Norms had crossed the creek and were fanning out on the opposite slope.

Then there was a faint rustle in the brush near him, up-creek, scant yards away. He twisted, ready to use his fists if he got the chance. The rustling came closer—and a big feline head poked into view. The beast eyed him as it crept closer.

His breath went out in a ragged sigh of relief as he recognized the cat. Dropping caution, he moved toward it; waited for it to turn and creep back the way it had come. He went to hands and knees to crawl along the twisting way it had found through the brush.

Ten minutes later he looked into the grinning blue face of Liss.

CHAPTER XIII: DESTINATION UNKNOWN

Murno turned his back on Kah Let and Kah Let's five nephews while he tried to master his rage. They waited patiently—as if, he thought darkly, he were a child.

They'd brought him to a small valley east of the lake, where, they said confidently, the Sierra Norms wouldn't look. A pile of knapsacks rested against a pine trunk; there were also a bow and some arrows and a knife to replace the ones he'd lost to the Norms. The sun was already down—they'd timed things, he suspected, so he wouldn't be able to refuse them and strike out west alone in the first explosion of his anger. Well, he wouldn't give them the satisfaction of shouting.

He spun to face Kah Let and said savagely, "The agreement was I'd rejoin my family, and talk to The Old One again!"

"That is true." Kah Let sounded honestly regretful. "And I've already told you The Old One says that if you insist, he'll hold to the agreement. But the situation's changed. To safeguard your family—as well as our own women and children—he's had to move them northward, hastily; and he's ready to move again if needful. Consider, Murno: the Gaddyl know for sure, now, that you reached the mountains, and they'll scour them looking for you. They don't know, though, that you brought your family all the way—remember, we planted false signs that they'd turned southwest instead of crossing the San Wah Keen with you. There's an excellent chance the deception will hold. Are you so anxious to reunite your family's destiny with yours? Would you not be a hazard to them?"

Murno snarled an oath. "What's the difference whether I go back or not? The Gaddyl will still be looking!"

"Well, perhaps not. Relatives of mine are at this moment constructing a false trail which Donnel will find in the morning. It leads south, along the eastern face of the mountains, then circles westward through a high pass—as if you were trying to rejoin your family somewhere in the Sack Toe Valley. Even if you refuse to accompany us east, that false trail may safeguard your family for a while. I tell you this, as proof that we are not trying to compel you."

Murno snorted. "There are other ways of compelling a man than by holding a knife against his navel! Why do *I* have to go, anyway? As long as *you're* going east, why don't *you* carry the contraband"—he toed the knapsack holding it—"and run down this 'Omha' legend?"

"Because—among other reasons—we may have to branch off on other pursuits. The Old One wants us to explore the Black Grove, for one thing—see if it might be a haven to which our people could migrate. And another reason is that we are mutants, and the subjects of many false rumors. We cannot travel among all Wild Folk." Kah Let watched Murno for a moment. "Do not worry that your family will misunderstand the necessity of your going without a farewell. The Old One is capable of explaining."

Murno laughed briefly and bitterly. "I'll concede that! And at the worst he could always just put them to sleep!"

The summit, with its harsh rocky peaks and dazzling snowfields, lay behind them. Murno slipped his backpack off and stretched out on his belly, under a bush, to peer eastward.

Two things were astounding—first, the nearly-bare, precipitately-plunging eastern face of the Sierra range; second, the dryness of the land below it. Mile after mile it stretched; low sandy bulges and dazzling salt flats, relieved only by a few insignificant creek-beds winding east from the mountains, and by a few bare isolated buttes. The maps, Murno recalled, had labelled the stretch "Rain Shadow." The term was appropriate.

Far to the northeast he could see a lake; another, about an equal distance southeast. Neither appeared to support much vegetation. Still, they'd have to be avoided; Gaddyl might go to either. In the east, hazy with distance, was an upthrusting of mountains, minor compared to the Sierras, that seemed to have some vegetation. And, beyond the mountains, on the eastern horizon—a long ways off, from this altitude—was a shimmery dark line broken only by a few peaks. Murno swept his eyes north and south along it. He could see no end.

Kah Let, on the other side of the bush, asked, "Is that the Black Grove?"

"I think so. I was flown around the northern edge once, but it's been years ago."

"Does it really stretch a thousand miles in every direction?"

Murno grunted. "I'd say the longest diameter would be a hundred-fifty."

Kah Let studied the landscape for a moment. "It does not look like an easy trip."

"It won't be," Murno told him, "but it's not impossible. Somewhere in that patch of mountains between here and the Grove is a small lake, and streams that feed it. The only worthwhile game is antelope. That draws a few Gaddyl. I don't know anything about the country from there to the Grove, but I suppose it's as dry as this below us." He stared eastward for a while. "We'll have to travel at night. I don't know where we'll hole up days. There'll be three, possibly four." He looked southward at the willow-lined creek nearest them. "That may be dry, but there's cover. I suggest we get to it and as far from the mountains as we can before dark."

For answer, Kah Let sang one of the high calls. Murno waited impatiently. Ten minutes later, the two felines came bounding toward them; then, one by one, from their various lookout-posts, Liss and his four cousins.

Two nights' travel (they spent the intervening day in the scant cover of a dry-wash) brought them to the minor mountain range. The western slopes were dry and rocky; the whole range, obviously, ancient and eroded. Nevertheless, within the chain there was greener country.

On the second morning, Murno sat with Liss on a moderate slope, in the cover of scrub pines, looking down into a north-and-south valley. A modest creek wriggled along it from the north, no doubt bound for the lake Murno remembered. The far slope and the country beyond looked green enough to hold game. Kah Let and the others had crossed over higher up, to scout the valley's main tributary from the east.

Murno glanced at Liss. "You're not cheerful."

The blue man peered south along the valley before answering. "There's a faint scent from the south that may be breloons. What would they be doing in this country?"

Murno futilely tested the breeze and squinted down-valley. "A party might be after bear or cougars, I suppose, or some other minor game they'd hunt in cover. Are you sure about the smell?"

"No." Liss stood up and began to move about restlessly. Murno divided his attention between the valley, the sky, and the mutant. Maybe they should move north, nearer where Kah Let had crossed over. He noted the blue man's increasing worry. It transferred to his own mind.

Suddenly Liss wheeled to face him. "Do you hear them?"

"No." Murno faced south and cupped his hands behind his ears.

It was five minutes before he heard, very faintly, a couple of barks. He got hastily to his feet. "Let's not be sitting here! Can you tell which side of the valley they're on?"

"The other side. Why don't you start north, Freed Man? I want a look at them. I'll catch you."

Murno looked at him unwillingly. "I don't want to leave you alone!"

Liss gave him a grin. "Go! I can outrun you by twice! Do you want me to have to slow my pace to yours?"

"Well . . . all right. I'll go straight along this slope." He turned; paused and looked at the blue man. "Can you warn Kah Let? Those talents of yours . . ."

"He has already felt my concern. But I must see them, really to . . ." He began muttering to himself, trying, Murno saw, to turn his attention inward.

Murno went north at the fastest jog he could hold.

The breloon sounds came closer—as Liss had said, up the other side of the valley. They weren't making much noise; just enough to communicate among themselves. No bellowing pack, this, mad with blood-lust and being deliberately noisy to panic the quarry; they were ranging easily along on some scent-trail hours old. When they sounded opposite he found a spot where he could see them bobbing along in a loose string. Thirty of them! There must be three Gaddyl parties or more camped at the lake, letting their beasts range casually. He scanned the sky anxiously. No geehawks. He started to run again. No hope of reaching Kah Let before the beasts picked up the blue men's trail. He caught glimpses of the brown bodies, drawing rapidly ahead of him. Then he saw the mouth of the canyon Kah Let had gone up. It was more heavily wooded than this valley. He saw the lead breloons pull up, circle for a minute, making sure of the trail and peering at the woods. A few yips, and the pack plunged in out of sight.

For a minute he heard them barking in the same tone. Then—abruptly—that changed. A frantic clamor broke out. There was a brief furious bedlam of snarls and shrieks that turned quickly into a screaming panic. Brown forms burst from the thicket in a disorganized rout. A few stragglers, shrilling in terror, humped frantically to catch up. One hobbled on three legs, throwing desperate looks behind him.

A light-furred form shot from cover and overtook the cripple in a few lightning bounds. There was a brief, contorting, screaming struggle and the feline leaped free. The breloon kicked a few times and went limp. The cat trotted back toward cover, paused to look over its shoulder, then slid out of sight.

Murno turned to see if Liss were coming yet. The young blue man stepped from behind a pine-trunk, grinning. "Let's cross over, Freed Man, while we can!"

83

The reunited party waded hastily up the tributary creek. Murno gasped between breaths, "How did you manage that?"

Kah Let told him, "We felt Liss' state of mind, and I could also sense that you were coming north on the other side of the valley. I could guess what was up long before we heard them, so we started back fast, and had time to get set. We started working at their minds, and as soon as they hesitated we hit them with darts. Then the cats charged. They probably saw the woods swarming with felines." He paused worriedly. "Will they run all the way back to their masters?"

"No. They wear radios, remember. Their handlers will meet them before they've gotten far. But they'll be little use for tracking, the rest of the day."

"Then, barring geehawks and aircars, we'll have time to construct trail puzzles and put some distance behind us?"

"That depends. There may be other breloons at the camp. Or they may fly in some, quickly." Murno peered around. "Hadn't we better get out of this canyon?"

Kah Let nodded. "At the first side-stream we'll make a false trail continuing up this one. I hope we can keep a good lead until night; there's high bare country to be crossed." He waded gloomily for a while. "We'll have more than Fiefdom Bay after us now, will we not, Freed Man?"

"Yes."

More silence. Then, "We must plan at least one day ahead. You say you've seen the north edge of the Black Grove. Do you think we should go around that way?"

"Definitely not! That's hunting country. We'd best go to the south, where it's too dry for much game."

CHAPTER XIV: THE BLACK GROVE

Murno peered through a screen of willows at the purpling sky. Two waves of geehawks had gone over during the afternoon, circling south. It was a disheartening thing—after two nights and two days of weary fleeing; of watching and scheming and making trail-puzzles.

Kah Let said, "It seems a long way to push a search, just

because of a few dead breloons. Are you sure they aren't from Fiefdom Bay?"

Murno sighed. "A long way? On foot, yes. How far do you think we've come, airline? Eighty miles? That's twenty minutes by aircar. They want to know what spooked a big pack of breloons. They know humans were involved somehow. You left darts in some of those carcasses."

Kah Let nodded. "I don't suppose they had to pick up the trail in more than a few spots, to know the general direction. Well, what now?"

"They'll be along and set down breloons on all the creeks coming east out of those mountains." Murno walked to where he could see in the other direction, east. A mile away, the stream vanished into the edge of the Black Grove. "If we're going into that thing, we'd better do it while there's still a little light. Maybe we can work south in the fringes."

"Correct." Kah Let came to his feet in one lithe motion. "Liss!" When the young man trotted into sight, Kah Let told him, "Murno and I are going ahead. We may try to go south under cover, but we won't go far until you catch up to us. The five of you and the cats stay here and construct a puzzle. After dark, unless something happens, head across country to that other creek we saw and try to make things look as if you'd headed back up it toward the mountains. Then come back to the edge of the Grove without leaving any trail."

Liss turned to go. Murno opened his mouth to protest, but Kah Let said quickly, "Those instruments you carry are important, remember?"

Murno mumbled his doubt, but Liss was already gone.

The last sunlight shone directly into the Grove, but it didn't get far.

At the edge, a few ordinary trees—pepperwood, for one—took advantage of what seemed to be an abrupt zone of richer soil, or moistness, to grow in a screen. A few yards in, the Grove proper assumed command.

There was only one species of tree, or several very similar species, with straight smooth-barked trunks as much as a yard thick that rose fifteen feet or more before suddenly branching in all directions to joust for space with

85

their neighbors. The leaves were round, from the size of a man's hand to a foot and more across, each on a stem like a length of wire that bent and curled to bring the leaf horizontal. Murno didn't realize what was so eerie about them until he looked straight up. The sky was completely obscured—as if by a solid roof—each leaf thrusting itself hungrily into position to gobble up any ray of light.

The effect, from the edge, was like peering into a cave. Murno stared at a leaf caught in a pencil of sunlight. It was a very dark green, and opaque.

He glanced at Kah Let. The blue man was rigid, listening. "What is it?"

Kah Let sighed. "Breloons, up the creek." He turned and took a few tentative steps into the Grove.

Murno said, "But, Liss hasn't had time to—"

Kah Let turned to him impatiently. "They've heard the beasts. They can take care of themselves; they'll have half an hour's grace. Come on! The darkness is to our advantage!"

For perhaps a hundred yards, enough light filtered in laterally so Murno could see the path they followed, and a few other things. He saw furtive flittings overhead—bats, maybe. The creek was already swallowed up beneath a lattice of great twisting roots that, to his imagining, might be giant snakes. The ground between treetrunks was bare, except for a low crinkly growth that might be a form of nettle. The trees bore no fruit that he could see. Here and there, slender shoots sprouted from the roots of old trees that looked ready to die.

It was an inhospitable-seeming place, and aside from the bats (if they were bats) he heard no sound of small creatures as in a normal forest. But where was the path Kah Let was leading him along so confidently? Now the light was gone; and he trod blindly, gingerly, able to proceed only because Kah Let (he was sure) deliberately set his feet down noisily. Shivers mounted his spine.

Somewhere outside the Grove, brelooms hallooed along the creek. They'd find no scent near the Grove—he and Kah Let had waded, of course—but would not their masters urge them in? Would there be flashlights?

After half an hour, Kah Let stopped. "I want to listen. And . . . there's an oddness. Can you feel it, Freed Man?"

Murno stood still. The air was moist, and warmer than he'd expect, and heady with a smell that reminded him of mushrooms. But . . . "Frankly, I feel so creepy, not being able to see, that I probably wouldn't know if I were walking through spiderwebs. I've been relying on your better senses. I mean, if there were carnivores . . ." He went silent, angry with himself for such a speech. "Why don't we turn south now?"

"For one reason, because there's no path. There's thick undergrowth now. For another, I don't know which way south is! We've twisted about; I can still hear the creek gurgling under its ceiling of roots, but it might be flowing in any direction. And I'm beginning to feel. . . . The edge of the Grove, Murno, was without animal life, except for those bats. Now—ahead and to the sides—I feel . . . life. Not danger. Just life. I want to go a little farther."

The breloon-cries had taken on a different note. Murno said distractedly, "I wonder if they've picked up Liss' scent. Can you—?"

Kah Let said, "Liss is moving, and he's alert, and he's involved in something, but he's not frightened. The trouble is . . . I find it hard to explain to you, a Normal. My sense of location relative to Liss is confused. This place diffuses it somehow!"

Murno let that pass. "Can you see at all?"

"Enough. Also, I can feel warmth from each tree-trunk, and avoid them that way. They have more warmth than pines have. That may be what makes the air feel different here." He was silent for a minute. "The Old One will want to experience this for himself!"

The distant breloon-cries reached a crescendo. And now Murno heard faint shouts, in Gaddyl. "I think the handlers are trying to urge the breloons in, but having trouble."

Kah Let chuckled. "I can feel the beasts' unwillingness. Come, Freed Man. Since I can feel life—and hear it too, now—in all directions, there must be other paths than this. Let us go a little farther."

But Kah Let led on only a hundred paces or so, before Murno, following by sound, heard him stop. There was silence. Then, to his astonishment, Kah Let sang a soft high note.

And—to his astonishment and fright—the note came

back as from a hundred throats all around them! He heard Kah Let gasp. The blue man said, "I can feel the trees! They're . . . sentient! And I've awakened them!"

Murno stood still, right hand stealing to his knife. He turned and blundered a few steps; crashed into thick brush—not the nettles he'd seen at the edge, but something chest-high and yielding.

Kah Let called sharply, "Murno!" Murno felt a familiar rigidness seize his muscles; half welcomed it; stood shaking.

And now the Grove took up the name, "Mur-no. Mur-no. Mur-mur-no-no-no." It echoed from all directions, receding in all directions, until it was a far-off whisper.

And, because there was in the tone only a sort of childish curiosity, some of his panic left him.

Kah Let found a path branching to the right, and led down it. Minutes later he stopped, and Murno heard sounds of a knife cutting something. A leather thong was thrust into his hand. "I'll tie the other end to my belt," Kah Let explained, "Then I can go quietly and you can still follow. We may have a chance of finding the edge. I can still feel Liss. He's searching—though I have no sense of his direction. I think . . . I think that the trees echo his feelings, as they echo mine, and my voice."

Murno felt the thong go taut. It was infinitely comforting—compared to walking completely blind—to be led thus. They walked for perhaps half an hour, making one sharp right turn. (How many gradual turns, he had no idea). Then the thong went slack again. He heard Kah Let inhale, and the mutant's voice sang out, "Liss! Liss!"

The trees took it up. "Liss. Liss. Ll-ll. Liss-iss-iss!" It echoed away on all sides. Then—after two full minutes—a whisper began; grew; rushed toward them: "Kah Let! Let-Let-Let!" Murno had a queer feeling that a great chorus was running by him, shouting—then the sound diminished in the opposite direction.

A moment later there rushed toward and by him a sound he recognized as the vastly-multiplicated nervous snarl of a feline. Kah Let cried out in excitement and delight, "We can tell direction of origin! It's like a light, radiating from a point!"

An hour later, Murno, sitting with brush at his back, blindly munching cold cooked meat, tried to puzzle out what the mutants were talking about. Kah Let came to his rescue. "You can not smell it, I know, Freed Man; but this Grove has another device that will thwart the breloons even if they can be urged in, with their handlers bearing lights. The trees have reproduced our scents! In all directions!"

That was too much to swallow. After a minute Murno said slowly, "There's never been any suggestion that the Black Grove was anything but a dense forest of a particular kind of tree. Gaddyl have hunted into the edges—even descended into the middle, with lights."

There was a thoughtful silence. After a while Kah Let said uncertainly, "There was no feel of sentience near the edge. And there was no voice reproduction, nor anything else of the sort, until I sang a command-note. I was trying to seize the minds of animals around us, thinking I might learn something of the Grove. So perhaps the Gaddyl never found anything of this."

"And perhaps," Murno said, his feelings in his voice, "they'll be along with bombs any minute."

There was a pause. Then Kah Let chuckled. "They'll have ample area to choose from, especially if we keep moving. I see no reason we should not continue on eastward. Shorter, since the Grove turns out to be passable after all, to go through than around."

"Huh." Murno felt a grim amusement. "So you've suddenly remembered which way's east? And what will we eat, when our food runs out? Bats?"

He heard Liss stir. Something cool and globular was thrust into his hands; something about the size of a grapefruit, and yielding. It smelled fruity. Kah Let said sharply, "Liss!"

"Oh, all right, Uncle." Liss sounded amused. "I'll try one first, myself. But you can see them all around you, some half-eaten on the bush. And consider—we've heard no sound of predation, though there are sounds of big animals, and smells. I say everything eats this!"

Kah Let said, "Nevertheless—" But there was already a biting sound. "Mm," Liss said, his mouth apparently full.

Murno, with an inward shrug, bit into his. Fruity, but more—somehow, robust and satisfying, like meat. He

89

finished it, then said resignedly, "All right, let's say we can live in this place for a few days. How about direction?"

"Why," Kah Let said, "I think we'll be able to see sun-direction, mornings and evenings. And—"

Abruptly, there was a snarl from the cats; gasps from the blue men. An instant later Murno gasped too.

A few yards along the path, a light was growing. A mere coal at first, it brightened; was joined by others in a cluster; glowed still brighter until it was almost like a candle-flame. Then, farther along the path, other clusters glowed into being. Murno scrambled to his feet, hand fumbling for his bow. Then he went rigid. Trees—half a dozen of them strung along the path——were producing the light.

The light came from clusters of objects the size and length of bananas, but straight, just below the branching of the trunks. That much he saw before the Grove around him burst into pandemonium.

A bat came jerkily at his head; swerved just in time; shot for darkness, squeaking rustily. Something big appeared in the path, stopped, staring toward the humans, said, "Woof!" in startled tones, and crashed away through the brush. At the edge of illumination, a deer leaped away, its eyes shining in the light for an instant as it looked back. Everywhere were squeaks and snarls and twitters.

But what really startled Murno was something that stepped from behind a tree and stared at him for an instant before turning to run. The body-shape was human, though small and spindly—but the ears were large as fans; the eyes huge and round. Murno heard the being's exclamation as it vanished—and in various directions, that exclamation was matched. He heard them fleeing through the brush, calling out to each other in voices that were ludicrously deep and a little blurred.

But they spoke English. And Gaddyl history told of such a mutation, long ago. It called them, simply, Big Ears.

There was only a minute until the startled exodus was over; then the Grove around them was utterly still. The cats crouched peering about nervously, ears drawn back, tails aflick. Kah Let said slowly, "I'll wager a dozen of these fruit growing around us that those trees will lead us east."

Startlingly, the lugubriously deep voice of a Big Ear came from the brush, perhaps thirty yards away: "Do not be so sure, Interlopers. The Gods of the Grove may be angry that you have awakened their trees!"

Somewhere above the Grove there was sunlight. Enough of it filtered down through the incredible foliage so that Murno could dimly see his companions, half-see trees and underbrush. No more trees glowed along the path—that had ceased with morning. Actually, he preferred this weaker light, because it was general, giving visual depth. He no longer felt pressed-in-upon.

Liss was the most talkative of the group. "I see no reason we could not live here! If the diet grew monotonous, we could venture out at night and hunt. At least, this could be a refuge for women and children. Personally, I would take delight in ranging out to see other lands and other peoples. Eastward, for instance, where the Orse pursue the great herds of bovines."

Kah Let said impatiently, "And how do you know we could stay healthy without the sun? In any case, our job is to explore, not to make decisions. And to get Murno safely past the Gaddyl search."

"Even so," Liss said, "on the way back—"

There was a sudden burst of light somewhere ahead. A moment later a shock wave struck—battering at Murno's ears; shoving him off balance; rattling through the Grove like a hurricane. Once again the Grove's furtive life exploded into panic. Now a second explosion rent the Grove in the other direction—then, in quick succession, four or five more, on all sides! Daylight filtered in from all directions except overhead.

As the brief bedlam faded, Gaddyl voices began to call back and forth. Kah Let seized Murno's arm. "Into the brush! My nephews will try—" Dazed, Murno let himself be tugged into cover. Obviously the Gaddyl had somehow pinpointed them! He fumbled at his pack; stopped. In this environment, arrows would be safer. He seized three from his quiver. He got his bow off his shoulders and squirmed into position to face the nearest source of light.

Somewhere a rifle cracked. Kah Let gasped, "One of us is hit!" A moment later Murno saw one of Kah Let's nephews steal hurriedly along the path they'd just quitted, hand clutching at his right bicep from which blood spilled. He passed from view—but a Gaddyl in guide's clothing appeared, a grimace of triumph on his face, and raised a short rapid-fire gun, to cut down the wounded mutant. Murno acted by reflex. He raised the bow, stepping a little to one side for room, drew, and shot. The arrow plunked into the alien's ribcase from the side. The scream of surprise and agony chopped off quickly. Now the shouts converged. There must be dozens of them! Murno had another arrow nocked; he was determined to take one more alien with him. Kah Let had the dart-thrower ready.

Four Gaddyl plunged into sight, weapons ready. And in that instant something rained down on them. He heard their screams before their guns fired wildly; saw them stagger and fall; heard the din of hammering guns and agonized yells from all sides. Heard, over all, a strange pelting as of big hailstones. Then—while he still stood with bow half-bent—the sound cut off. Now there was nothing but a few last groans.

It took him a minute to realize what he'd actually seen. From the trees, scores, hundreds, of the banana-sized things—the same kind that had glowed with light, so far as he could tell—had twisted themselves to aim, then elongated themselves like vastly-powerful springs suddenly released, to fly free and true, faster than any arrow! He could see them now, everywhere, plunged half their elongated lengths into the ground or impaling Gaddyl corpses.

Minutes must have passed before he moved. By that time Liss—for once, looking shaken—was trotting into sight. Shortly, his cousins, including the wounded one, appeared too. The cats slunk into sight, heads lowered nervously.

Before anyone spoke, a voice came from a tree thirty yards away. "Mur-no. Liss. Kah-Let." It was a deep voice, though not so deep as the voices of Big Ears; a little labored. "Take alien weapons you can use, but only a few. Leave no sign of yourselves. Hurry eastward as the trees guide—my people will police up here, so the real story of this fight cannot be read. I will talk to you later!"

CHAPTER XV: THE FULL BLUE

Something like a hundred hours had passed since the slaughter of the Gaddyl. Murno felt he and his companions must be nearing the eastern edge of the Grove. He'd lost most of his fear, now, of the weird forest. As to their mysterious host—well, if that being had so wished, he could have killed them at any moment.

They'd passed more than one old wound in the Grove, where Gaddyl had blasted their ways in at some time or other; perhaps out of simple curiosity. There'd been other places where they saw daylight, too—around buttes that reared up through the canopy. They'd climbed one of those for a look around, seen a few aircars going over high up, but no sign of trouble. Maybe the dead Gaddyl hadn't yet been found. Their host wasn't talking.

It was as they neared another break (as always, the path split, with one branch detouring widely) that their host did speak again, via the trees. "This is a real mountain you're approaching. The path you're on will cross a stream. Go up it, and I'll meet you."

They made a common halt, looking at each other. Murno's stomach was knotting. He hesitated, shrugged, and started on.

They found the stream and turned up it; left the trees of the Grove and were in normal-looking pine forest—there were even jays and squirrels to scold at them. The feel of open air was wonderful.

A few yards more, and someone suddenly said, "Hello.' It was recognizably the voice of the trees, without the labored quality. Murno stood, pulse hammering, and watched a huge man come toward them. At the same time that he felt relief because their host was human, awe, so intense as to be almost panic, rippled up his spine. He heard his companions let out their breaths raggedly. The cats let out subdued little snarls.

Their host's skin was blue.

This blue man was to The Old One as The Old One was to, say, Kah Let. He was huge, and he was old, and he was mighty, with no hint of senility. His skin—darker blue than The Old One's—was like the hide of an old buck deer. It was crisscrossed with ancient scars, healed to insignificance. As one big hand rested for a moment on a pine-trunk, Murno saw that half the little finger was gone.

So, this—the master of the Black Grove—was after all no God.

The being gave the cats a casual glance that seemed to quiet them, then smiled at Kah Let. "If you're thinking that you and I are relatives, you're right. That much I knew when my trees first responded to you at the western edge of the Grove. I was not entirely surprised. Of late, I have been feeling a thought from beyond the Sierras —a probe from someone less ancient than I, yet centuries old. I think that you come from him."

Kah Let sounded like a child confronting a stern elder. "It's The Old One whose probe you feel. He is—I think he must be a—a nephew of yours. Legend says—" He ran out of words.

The huge mutant nodded. "I schemed very hard to establish that error. As you can see, I did not die. The deception has held. Even the Big Ears, who know me somewhat, do not guess my history—their eyes could not, in any case, distinguish the color of my skin." He shook his head sadly. "I've sent them scattering from the spot of your near-ambush. I hope they'll obey; they're simple folk, and gentle. I must flee too—I cannot depend upon fooling the Gaddyl this time. I will turn off the Grove, and go elsewhere."

Kah Let said wonderingly, "You control trees more completely than we control animals!"

The big head nodded. "That was the Gaddyl's intent, in the original experiment—we were to be gardeners. But they unlocked far more than they knew existed." He smiled. "Strange, is it not—I have no power with animals, while you hybrids have no power with plants! It hints at deeper secrets."

Kah Let asked humbly, "You've known of us, then?"

"Yes, vaguely—a few half-sentient trees, descended from my first experiments, grow in your country. Then, of course, rumors do spread. I have my ears in various places." He glanced, perhaps involuntarily, at a patch of sky. "I do feel directly the mind of your Old One, and, faintly, your own. I know you are troubled, and of course I know why."

Kah Let took a deep breath and said hurriedly, "The Old One will want to meet you! And as your refuge here is unsafe now, why do you not return with us to the Sierras? There are wild mountains in the north where we may find safety." He hesitated. "We are half blue. The talents fade. Whereas—were you to mate with one of our women——."

The huge blue being chuckled deeply. "I assure you, at my age curiosity would be the main goad. I have had mates—centuries past—but no children survive now. And burying so many, one grows reluctant . . ." He seemed to shrug off the past, and looked suddenly at Murno. "But you have been speaking, along the way, of a need to escort this Freed Man eastward. How, then, do you speak of turning back?"

Kah Let said, "I have not considered . . . that is, perhaps some of us . . ."

Murno, a little over his first awe, felt a stirring of new excitement. "There's one specific reason for my going east. You are—you have a memory over a thousand years old! Tell me—have you ever heard the name, 'Omha'?"

The blue being smiled. " 'Omha Abides!' That legend was strong, in my youth. Perhaps, as with many legends, its only strength lay in its believers. It is nearly dead now."

Murno stared at him for a moment, an odd hollowness growing inside him. "Then . . . there was never anything in it?"

The blue man shrugged. "I did not say that. Its beginning was before mine. But there is only one tribe, so far as I know, who still believe—the Burnies. They are far east of here, in a range of mountains called The Rockies."

Murno struggled with emotions he did not understand. "I don't know whether I—"

The full-blooded blue mutant looked at him directly. "Have you a definite mission?"

"Well . . . yes. Some instruments I'm carrying."

"Oh." The big face went thoughtful. "You are not the first. Through the generations, there have been others. Well—I cannot decide for you, Normal. But if you wish to go on, I can advise you how."

Murno stood silent and miserable. He wanted, more than anything, to get back to his family. Yet the arguments against that, for what they meant, still held. And he could not say that he cared nothing about the mission. If there were any chance, even the tiniest, to strike a blow against the Gaddyl, he wanted to do it. He realized, suddenly, that he *ached* to do that. When had this obsession begun? He could not tell. But so many had died to speed the stolen instruments on their way. . . . Perhaps it was that. Simply to give up now would be a betrayal of all those martyrs. And so far as his doubts about "Omha" were concerned—how could he know what might exist somewhere? Had he not already, in a few short weeks, seen things he would have called utterly fantastic before? He sighed. "How would I go?"

The mutant's eyes rested on the hunting-rifle Murno had appropriated from a slain Gaddyl. "The Orse are jealous of their lands, and do not welcome strangers. But that rifle you have would be an impressive fee. They are fiercely honorable, within their code, and loyal to their friends. And they travel fast. Have you ever ridden a horse?"

"No."

"Well, you can learn. Your friends and I could escort you to the edge of the Grove, if you felt able to go on alone. It's open country such as you crossed to get here, and you'd need the good will of the Orse to cross it. I'm not sure they'd extend that to your blue-skinned companions here."

"Well . . ." Murno hesitated miserably. "As I remember, the Rockies are far beyond this Grove."

"Far, yes. But a mounted man might find it a reasonable trip."

Murno drew a deep breath. He looked at his companions. "Without me, you could get back to the Sierras a lot faster. And I'd rather have you there, looking after my family if they need it, than somewhere along the way looking after me."

Oory sat rigid in his aircar as it hovered under control of Ingress Traffic Monitor. There'd be no courtesies for him this time. The abrupt summons to Occupation Headquarters hadn't even born Stolm's signature. In any case, he would not embarrass his ex-friend by mentioning his name.

There was no doubt in his mind that he faced bad trouble.

A red light winked on the control panel and the car dropped, checked, settled to the pavement. A spotlight stabbed at him. A Squad Prime and four Armsmen, wearing handguns, marched up and stood waiting. He slid back the canopy and climbed out; felt a stir of anger as the five didn't even dip their heads. Was he, then, stripped of all rank without even a hearing?

The Squad Prime said formally, "This way, please, Visitor."

The Council was in a small room, with a single long table at which sat eight Fiefs, all of whom Oory knew. None of them gave him a glance except Guddun, who let one cold look flick over him. He stepped to the side of the door and inclined his head correctly.

The Squad Prime who'd escorted him said, "Sire . . . Your Primacy . . . Your Eminence . . . [that last for Elzewain, who stood at Stolm's shoulder] I bring as ordered Visitor Oory, formerly of Fiefdom Bay."

None of the Fiefs deigned to acknowledge. Elzewain said, "We take note, Squad Prime. You may leave."

The eight Fiefs sat alone one side of the table, facing Stolm. Some of them toyed with hors d' oeuvres or sipped from ornate glasses. Their expressions ranged from boredom to Guddun's frozen anger. Evidently they'd been having words among themselves, or with Stolm.

Stolm, without glancing at Oory, said, "May we now, Sirs, hear testimony from the former Chief-At-Arms of Fiefdom Bay?"

There were a couple of "yesses" and a few shrugs. An

old Fief at the opposite end from Guddun (who, as least senior, sat at the far left) said, "If I may, Commandant, I'll open the questioning."

"Of course, Fief Hettel."

Hettel glanced at Oory as impersonally as if they'd never met before. "We have heard, Armsman, that prior to your removal as Fief Guddun's Chief-At-Arms—let me express, by the way, my disapproval that you have not had any notification—you were conducting a search for a runaway slave called Murno."

Oory fought to keep his face expressionless. Bad enough to learn thus publicly that he was stripped clear down to Armsman, without the additional disgrace of losing dignity before so many Fiefs. He inclined his head and spoke as calmly as he could. "An em, Elder sir. He received his manumission from Fief Kokiel nearly fourteen years ago."

Guddun glared hate. Hettel waved an impatient hand. "An em, then. His initial crime was in aiding slaves to escape, and in receiving stolen instruments?"

Oory hesitated. The articles he'd recovered from Donnel of the Sierra Norms were *not* the items he'd sought. But without understanding more of that, he'd better not mention it. "Those were possible crimes of his, Elder Sir. There is no direct evidence. But there's persuasive evidence that he participated in the . . . murder . . ." Oory stumbled over the word, "of two Gaddyl guests and a guide. And it's certain he was involved in an organization of ems who did help the escapees, and who had done similar things before."

Guddun burst out, "My father was an utter fool in his policies toward ems!"

Hettel glared once at Guddun, then faced Oory again. "Your former Fief informs us that your efforts to capture this slave, or em, were exceptionally inept. Would you agree?"

Oory dipped his head to hide his face for a moment. "Naturally I cannot disagree, Elder Sir. I almost had him, and perhaps it was some ineptness of mine, rather than the Will of Fortune, or Murno's cleverness, that let him slip the trap. All I can say now is that he is probably alone in very difficult country, surrounded by humans who will hardly be hospitable." He hesitated. "If the search be pushed—."

Hettel stared him in the eye. "I'm glad you admit ineptness. For this slippery em is *not* bottled up west of the Sierra summit as you evidently believe." The old Fief glanced around at his fellows. "Have I your permission, Sirs, to speak of the Black Grove affair?"

A Fief near the middle of the table said, "Why not? It'll soon enough be gossip at every swimming-puddle, anyway."

Hettel grunted an acknowledgement. "You've seen the Grove, Armsman?"

Oory made an affirmative bow.

Hettel went on, "It seems none of us had looked closely enough at it. A hunting party chased a small group of humans and trained animals who'd ambushed and routed a band of breloons. The quarry reached the Grove—no minor feat, considering the terrain—and took refuge in it. Scouts, probing in, heard a considerable body of men calling out this Murno's name, as if it were a rallying-cry. Tracking the band from the air above the Grove, using sensitive sound-pickups, the hunting party, with borrowed reinforcements—including a dozen of my own security guards—surrounded it and blasted a way in." Hettel paused. "They were wiped out, so quickly they could not even get one aircar aloft nor radio a description of the weapons or tactics." He grinned icily. "Perhaps, Armsman, we are uncharitable in calling you inept. This Murno seems to have followers, and far more than his share of sagacity."

Guddun broke in nastily, "What are we learning that we didn't know an hour past? The purpose of this Council is not to discuss the hunting down of a particular lucky fugitive. Let Stolm worry about that—clearly, it's become a job for Occupation now. *We* have a proposition to vote on. Let's do it!"

There were grunts of agreement from several others.

"Very well," Hettel said. "As Senior, I choose to vote last. Guddun?"

"My own vote, and four proxies from North Am continent: Yes!"

"Chunn?"

"My vote, and six proxies from South Am. Yes."

"Hwilz?"

"Four proxies from Affreek, plus my vote. Yes."

Hettel said, "That is already a majority, Sirs. Shall we make it unanimous?"

"Unanimous."

"Unanimous."

When all others had agreed, Hettel said, "I vote unanimity, with reservations: I will continue the old restrictions in my own Fiefdom. Commandant Stolm, I'm sure you will handle the formalities with complete thoroughness, but will you state the approved proposition formally for us now?"

Stolm said tonelessly, "It is voted by the Council of Fiefs of the planet Earth, that, various aborigines both in slavery and out, having committed willful murders of Gaddyl, the agreement against hunting humans, normal or mutant, for sport, is ended. Vote audited and attested by Occupation Command, not concurring in the affirmative vote but bowing to the decision of the Council."

Hettel showed his teeth in a yawn. "Fine. We can adjourn now, I hope."

Stolm said casually, "There is one small item, Sirs. I have already messaged off-planet that Armsman Oory here, having been duly stripped of rank for cause, will remain for the time being attached to Occupation for possible usefulness. May I have the formality of your votes?"

Guddun, snarling, was on his feet. "You had no right to do that! He's still in the service of Bay!"

Stolm looked surprised. "Why, Young Sir, I had no idea . . . there's clear precedent that when a Fief asks Occupation to strip anyone in Category Arms of rank, that person is ousted from the Fiefdom and reverts to Occupation!"

Hettel broke·in testily, "For Hereafter's sake, Guddun, let the fellow be! One would almost suspect you wanted to hush him up for some reason. I vote approval of Stolm's action!"

Others chorused agreement. Guddun, face suffused with blood, subsided into his chair.

Oory, mortified at the exchange, stood as inconspicuously as possible against the wall while the Fiefs filed out. His mind was racing. Clearly, the loss of the Distorter still was not common knowledge among the Fiefs, and Guddun didn't want it to be—even with Oory blamed.

Stolm had undoubtedly just saved Oory's life.

When the Fiefs were gone and Oory faced Stolm alone, there was, of course, no informality. Stolm said, "I've inherited a problem, as you've heard, and your acquaintance with this Murno qualifies you to work on it. I'm giving you the temporary rank of Company Prime. You'll have six tens of Armsmen, with aircars and equipment, and your central task will be to catch Murno and his renegades. The recovery of the stolen items, which we will not mention publicly, will, one presumes, follow as a matter of course."

In the existing circumstances, it would be improper for Oory to express the gratitude that constricted his throat. When he could speak calmly, he said, "I will serve to my utmost." He hesitated. "May I speak, Your Primacy?"

"Speak."

"Primacy, there are twenty-five million humans in North Am. Hardly more than a handful own firearms, but as this affair has shown, they cannot be discounted as fighters. And with blood-thirsty sportsmen swarming here to hunt them—that will happen, as certainly as sunrise—there'll be general uprisings. I urge you to message off-planet for more Garrison personnel—real Armsmen—and for a flotilla or two of fighting ships!"

Stolm's nictating membranes slid over his eyes for a second. "Between you and Guddun, you'd have me making a complete fool of myself. Do you think I like this hunting of humans, or intend merely to shrug it off? In dealing with Fiefs, Armsman, indirect methods must often be used. Let a few guests get themselves ambushed here and there—let the Fiefs be hit with some real indemnity claims—and they'll be anxious to reverse their votes!"

Oory said, "Primacy, I'm concerned with more than a few ambushed guests or lawsuits."

Stolm showed his teeth scornfully. "You think we'll see armies marching against Fiefdoms? Or perhaps against Ingress itself? You're overwrought, Armsman—understandably. You may withdraw now. The Quartermaster will assign you suitable rooms. I want you out scouting first thing in the morning!"

Cheeks muddy with humiliation, Oory made the proper

bow and left the chamber. So his ex-friend thought he was hysterical! Well, events would show!

The room was utilitarian; unadorned, as befitted a mere Company Prime. There was no private pool, of course—only a shower. He slumped on a pad, leaning his head back against the wall, eyes shut.

He wondered how his family was. He hoped they wouldn't abandon dignity and try to see him, after this disgrace—but probably Stolm would have the decency to forestall that. Maybe his ex-friend would even arrange for him to hear news of them, if it were good.

"Kokiel, Kokiel," he murmured, "I have not turned upon your son, nor will I. But how alone I am."

CHAPTER XVII: THE ORSE

Murno crouched among willows, wishing one of the blue men were here to sniff the air and identify the infinitesimal taint that had sent him to cover so soon after leaving the eastern edge of the Grove. A burnt smell—ashes? Something more. And another smell, like freshly-cut iron just beginning to rust—or—blood.

The small life along the creek didn't show any fright. Carefully, he moved from cover and started up the small creek. The smell strengthened. In ten more minutes he found the source.

There'd been a campfire in a cleared space on the south bank of the stream. Obviously, the spot had been used often—there were weathered lengths of log angled around the circle of blackened stone, for seats. The most recent fire was ashes. The haunch of meat spitted above them was scorched black on the bottom, still raw—and covered with flies—on top.

The woman who should have turned the spit lay face down, one braid of her long brown hair half burned away where it had fallen into the fire. Her leather garment, a one-piece dress, was also burnt on that side. Her blood had made a pool on the hard-packed ground, and congealed. Flies crawled and swarmed.

Cautiously, Murno began to scout the area.

The man lay fifty yards up-creek, where he'd been gathering firewood. He'd gotten his bow into action; it was still clutched in his right hand. A bullet had entered his chest, from high up on the right side; another had struck his right shoulder at such an angle that his arm must have been upraised—as if he'd been aiming almost vertically. The arrow wasn't in sight.

There was no telling whether he or the woman had been killed first, but obviously neither had had more than an instant's warning. An aircar, then, must have swooped along the creek, taking quick pot-shots. Murno wondered whether there'd been other people camped there.

He found signs of one more. Out in the grass, three horses had been tethered to simple willow-wands thrust into the ground. The freshest set of human footprints led from a thicket near the camp to the tethering-spot, and the horses' trails led from there southeast: They'd been running all-out. He could not tell whether the survivor was a girl or a boy, but it was a child not much over ten, he'd guess. He backtracked to the thicket, where he found a fishing-pole. The child had left tracks as he or she wandered aimlessly in the willows, perhaps weeping blindly, for a while; then had gone to the horses, mounted one, and led the other two along.

The whole layout made him think the trio had been on a casual trip—possibly, he thought, to show the youngster the Black Grove.

He went back to the dead woman, turned her over and noted the same downward angle of the bullets. Murno carried her under some willows and laid her down. He got mud to plaster over her wounds and the blood on her garment, because it bothered him to see the flies swarming on her, then he went after the man and brought him to lie beside the woman. He plastered his wounds too. Finally he scanned the sky without seeing geehawks or aircars, walked about making a trail-puzzle in case breloons came, and chose a hiding-place. He thought that very probably humans would be along after dark.

They came an hour after sundown; eight mounted men, four in single file on each side of the creek, riding cautiously. He waited for them to dismount, satisfy themselves there was no Gaddyl ambush, gather, and find the two bodies. There was a minute of puzzled talk, then they all went silent, hands stealing toward knives. Once they had the realization that someone had moved the bodies, he felt ready to show himself. "Hello." He left his concealment; walked into sight so they could inspect him.

Their garments were leather, pretty much like his own. They wore moccasins, not boots; had big knives in scabbards; carried bows in their left hands, along with three or four arrows apiece. Their hair was long, in two braids, like that of the dead man and woman. They were all deeply tanned, if not actually swarthy, with deepset eyes that looked dark in the starlight.

They surveyed him silently for a while, then one spoke. "Did you see it happen?"

"No. I came along about mid-afternoon. They'd been dead for hours."

"Why'd you daub mud on them? And move them?"

"I put them out of sight in case the Gaddyl came back. If they saw the bodies still there, they might decide to set an ambush. I used the mud because it bothered me to see flies on them. Maybe that's silly."

The spokesman thought things over. "Good sense, about the Gaddyl." He walked slowly to the fire-spot and peered at it. "You've been here since mid-afternoon but you didn't take any of the meat."

"Well . . . I guess it didn't occur to me, the way things were. I don't know the customs here but to me it would seem a little wrong."

"I see. Well, fellow, you did what you could for them, so by our customs you can eat the meat. We're going to. You can take a turn with us digging graves, if it'll make you feel better. Then we'll eat, and you can clear out. Ordinarily we don't encourage strangers to stay. What were you doing here, anyway?"

There were a few grim chuckles. The spokesman said, "Just like that, eh? Where'd you come from?"

Murno hesitated. "From . . . west of the Grove."

Somebody snorted in doubt. "Which way'd you come around? North or south?"

Murno was getting tired of the questions, but he'd better not admit he'd come *through* the Grove. "I sure didn't come around the North—that's popular Gaddyl hunting country. Do you object to strangers just crossing your land?"

More chuckles. "We usually object pretty hard."

Murno, a little heat in his voice, said, "Well, I'll introduce myself, anyway. My name's Murno. I'm an em, from Fiefdom Bay, and I've got business somewhere east, with a tribe called the Burnies. And I've got something to trade you for permission to cross your precious land. I didn't think it was the right time to start bargaining."

The spokesman said, "Look, fellow. You did the decent things, and now we'll bury these two, and their son will be looked after. But no amount of piousness will bring them back to life. What is it you brought to trade?"

"It's in the brush." Murno went and got the Gaddyl rifle; handed it to the spokesman. "There are three dozen cartridges in it; high velocity, thin profile; a synthetic metal twice as heavy as lead. I've got four more clips in my pack, of three dozen each. Will that buy my way across?"

The group gathered excitedly around the weapon. Presently the spokesman left the group. "It'll do. Were you figuring to go on foot?"

"I got this far on foot."

"Huh. It's a lot farther to the Burnies. You'd better join up with us for a while. We've got an extra horse with us we were going to load this couple's stuff on, but we can distribute it. My name's Larkan." He offered a hand.

After handshakes all around, Larkan told one of the others, "Dal, get the shovels and let's get it over with."

Murno's first sight of the clan (of which Larkan, it seemed, was leader) came a little after midnight. The campfires, several dozen, made a necklace around the base of a hill that loomed, jagged-topped, against the stars. The tents were of various kinds, from simple teepees to tents with fifteen-foot lodgepoles, guyed to stakes. A few men—perhaps on watch—sat around the fires.

Larkan slowed his horse to let Murno come alongside. "Got the hang of riding yet?"

105

"Frankly, no. When the horse comes up, I always seem to be going down, and vice versa. I don't think I'll sit down again for a week."

Larkan chuckled. "We've only been trotting, in case of gopher-holes. Wait until you try a rough-gaited stallion at a full gallop!" He was silent for a minute. "You came from Bay. Is there trouble there too?"

Murno's mind worked fast. He hated being an hypocrite with these people, but he wouldn't accomplish anything by getting himself, possibly, blamed for their trouble. "Bad trouble out there. How long's it been going on here?"

Larkan said, "The first was a month ago, when they took pot-shots at a couple of hunters. There've been half a dozen incidents since then. One was a killing that may have come from an argument over a carcass. This is the first thing like this."

Murno felt a little less guilty. He said, "Things may be related. There's a new Fief of Bay, and he's broken the old agreement. These could be some of his guests you've had trouble with."

"Mm." The clan leader was thoughtful for a while, then, "I'm going to have to ask you a few more questions. About your business with the Burnies, for one thing."

Murno had already decided he could talk about that. "In my pack are three items stolen from Bay. I didn't steal them but I'm saddled with the job of transporting them, like this horse is saddled—without being asked in advance. One's a Gaddyl handgun. You couldn't use that without bringing Gaddyl down on you fast; it lets out a burst of static any radio can hear. The other two are instruments of some kind that you couldn't use either. I may be chasing a myth, but I'm going to try to catch it. There's a password . . . 'Omha Abides!' "

Larkan grunted. "The Burnies are the people for you, then. I've never been that far east myself, but I've known people who have. The only thing is, you may have trouble finding the Burnies. They're seclusive as hell."

Murno said, "I have to try. Could you give me some kind of letter to help out? I understand there are a lot of clans between here and the Rockies."

"A lot," Larkan affirmed. "You'll be a few days learning to ride well enough, anyway, and learning the country, so I think you ought to stop over with us. Also, I want to ask you more about the Gaddyl." He paused. "You say you're an em. You don't happen to understand any Gaddyl, do you?"

Murno told him, "I grew up in the personal service of a Fief and his household. I speak Gaddyl as well as I speak English."

The Orse leader went rigid; reined closer and seized Murno's forearm. "Listen, Freed Man—we've got a few radios we've found here and there! How long would it take you to teach us enough Gaddyl so we could hear what was going on?"

Murno considered that unhappily. "Well—about as long as it'll take me to learn to ride."

Larkan chuckled. "It's a bargain. But I've got one other thing on my mind first. I've got to move the clan to cover."

With first light, the moving of camp began. The creek along which Murno had emerged from the Grove, many miles west, flowed around the opposite side of this hill. While it wasn't much, it had the only cover nearby.

The Orse seemed not to know much about cover. Murno told them, "Get your children over there first. Then start on the smallest tents. You won't be able to hide these bigger ones anyway." He stared dubiously along the string of fires. "You're going to have to change a lot of habits. Aren't there any pine forests anywhere near?"

Larkan scowled. "What wooded country there is, everybody will be heading for, if it comes to that."

Murno pondered. "Well, you'll have to make yourselves harder to find, one way or another. Hole up during the day; hunt at night. The more trouble it is for them, the fewer of them will think it's worth-while. It's possible this thing may be only temporary. The other Fiefs may demand a stop. In the past there's been a heavy majority against it."

Larkan eyed him. "And if it's not temporary?"

"Well"— Murno squirmed mentally—"I'm not sure there's a good answer to that."

Larkan snarled an oath. "I'll tell you this much, Freed Man—we're not sheep!"

After breakfast Murno took one of the small Gaddyl

radios his hosts possessed, and climbed the hill, on the theory that he was the best suited lookout.

The land rolled gently on and on, with only a few widely-spaced hills like this one, sliced by a few creeks from the east. Grass was rather sparse, and already bleached to straw. The Grove—which seemed to swallow up all the creeks within sight—looked surprisingly close in the clear air. He saw no activity over it. The spot of the fantastic massacre, of course, was too far away to see aircars, if any.

From the north brow of the hill he could see what he first took for brushland—until he realized it was slowly shifting. Bison, then; a big herd; tens of thousands. Northeast, not so far away, was a small herd of the long-horned cattle; beyond, a fast-moving dust-cloud that might be horses on the run. The cloud swerved, and he saw a glint in the air above it—some aircar out on an early hunt. Probably, all across the wide land that was going on. How many beasts were slaughtered in a day—how many Gaddyl rifles fired?

Enough, if other Fiefs followed Guddun's example and allowed hunting of humans, to keep a lot of Wild Folk busy with shovels.

He tried to push that thought away, but it wouldn't stay pushed. And in mid-morning he heard an exchange on the radio that brought it back for good:

"Guide Eleven Nineteen: This is Eleven Eight. Did you get your equines?"

"Eleven Eight: Yes. Each of my guests got a fine stallion. How is *your* hunt?"

"So-so. A long-horn apiece, and we landed to get the heads. We're going now to have a look at that camp of Wild Folk we saw from a distance. Do you want to join us?"

There was a pause; then, "Eleven Eight: My guests want to know if you're going to do any shooting."

"Eleven Nineteen: Not unless they show fight, or we see a particularly good specimen. My guests just want to see what the aborigines look like."

"Eleven Eight: We'll join you, but let's stay at a safe altitude. Remember that affair in the Grove!"

"Eleven Nineteen: Those weren't Orse—it was that

renegade from Bay, with his band of hostiles. But we'll be careful."

Murno stood for a moment, aghast at the various implications; then turned and ran toward the opposite brow of the hill. He shouted and waved to the Orse still working around the old camp. It seemed incredibly long before they looked up. He pointed urgently at the sky. For a minute they stood staring up at him, then they burst into action. The few women still there were herded into the remaining tents. Most of the men followed them. Two men sprinted toward picketed horses; leaped upon them and headed around the hill at a dead run.

By the time the first aircar came into sight, the camp looked deserted. There were no horses—all those were already around the hill. Murno, hidden among rocks, watched the second aircar arrive. There was no talk on the radio; the two hovered side by side, canopies open, so they could talk back and forth. Presently the cars moved off eastward. But as they started, one guest—from pure spite, perhaps—let loose four quick shots at the biggest tent still standing.

Murno scrambled to his feet and plunged down the hill as fast as he could. By the time he reached the tent, two men were carrying a woman from it. She was still alive, but unconscious and obviously dying.

The men stood staring down, while one tried to stop her bleeding. Finally one said in a choked, incredulous voice, "She didn't let out a murmur. Just gritted her teeth and laid there."

Murno, Larkan, and a few others squatted near the creek. Larkan's voice was flat and hard. "I don't want to listen to any more talk now about how to hide ourselves. The women can work that out." He stared straight at Murno. "How can we hurt the Gaddyl, with what we've got? Hit-and-run raids on swimming places? Ambush them when they land to take trophies?"

Dal—a young man with light eyes—burst out, "Hell! Hit a Fiefdom!"

Murno said slowly, "The hit-and-run, and the ambush, you can try with some chance of success. Stay away from the Fiefdoms. They've got concentrated firepower there."

Larkan nodded shortly. "Sure. But there are a lot of us. And we'd just as soon die in bunches, fighting, as be picked off a few at a time. You say they don't have many actual soldiers on Earth. How long would it take them to get reinforcements from off-planet!"

"Not much longer than it would take an Armsman to pack his stuff and climb into a ship. Translocation from the nearest other Gaddyl-occupied planets is less than an hour."

Dal put in, "But they'd all have to come through Ingress—is that right?"

Murno told him impatiently, "It would be twelve or fifteen years without the Translocation Center. But if you're thinking you could knock that out, stop wasting your brains. The Gaddyl have had native rebellions on more than one world. They know how to build a strong point and hold it. Ingress is also Occupation Headquarters, you know."

Larkan asked, "You've seen it?"

"Once, years ago."

Larkan got to his feet and took a few restless steps. "Still, that's one of the things we ought to think about— and talk about with other clans. Are you still determined to go east?"

Murno said, "I'm not going to do the Gaddyl much harm loafing around here."

"All right," Larkan said, "a few more days, to teach us a little Gaddyl and to get used to horses. Then, suppose I send a few men with you, as a sort of envoy party. Will you tell other clan leaders what you know about the Gaddyl?"

"Of course."

A man with a beard more grizzled than Murno's—and with the only cloth shirt in the group—said, "I know quite a few of the clans east of here. And I've been to the Rockies."

Larkan said, "All right, Parks. You and Dal and about three others. A couple of extra horses to carry supplies."

Eleven days, or twelve—he wasn't sure—had passed since Murno and several companions left Larkan and started east.

The mountain near the peak of which he stood now was higher than anything for a good many miles ahead. With him were Parks—who'd showed a good acquaintance with the country so far—and a young man named Wing they'd added to the party along the way; a member of a clan they'd found in disorganized flight. That clan—led by a man named Sanders—was only one of several they'd met, and advised, and conscripted into Larkan's tentative confederation. Dal and the rest of the party were lower down the mountain, with the horses.

Parks said, "I thought the view would be worth the climb. Do you recognize anything you ever flew over?"

Murno shook his head. "Not exactly. We crossed the canyon farther down, where it runs from east to west before turning south again. We were flying almost a straight line from Bay to Ingress. I remember, though, that on the maps, the river above that famous part of the canyon comes from north-east. I can just about place the stretch we're looking at."

Wing said, "It's a real canyon you're looking at, too. And plenty of side canyons."

"I'll agree with that," Parks said. "Murno, where's Ingress from here? Southeast?"

"No—we've already passed it. A couple hundred miles south and a little west, I'd say. It's in mountains that get a lot more rain than what we've been crossing." This range had surprised Murno—he'd had no idea it was so rugged. And there was game enough to feed the clans now taking hurried refuge here, if they could adapt quickly to new ways of hunting.

He turned and looked north. There were peaks there too; hazy and shimmery in the noon heat. "Somewhere up that way," he told his companions, "is a big lake of salt water. The Gaddyl visit it as a curiosity, but the climate's too hot to suit them. Farther north is a small Fiefdom."

Wing said, "There are supposed to be Orse clans up that way."

Murno nodded. He looked east again toward the irregular dark line in the distance, angling across their path. "We might be able to get across that before tonight's over."

"No," Wing said. "Aircars fly up and down it all day, and a lot of them turn up side canyons, and some camp overnight. We can get fairly close tonight, but we'll have to hole up tomorrow. Then the next evening we can scout the main canyon, and cross over right after dark. Then we'll be well beyond by morning."

Murno accepted that silently. It seemed years he'd been travelling eastward, and always it was caution and delay and detour. How long had it been, really? Hardly more than a month?

The tributary canyon they'd followed down from the mountains curved more and more to the right as they approached the main one, until now it ran almost south. Wing said it was puny compared to what they'd be crossing, but Murno found it awesome enough. Here, near its mouth, it was over a mile wide—a vertical-walled cleft with a broken bottomland through which the small river ran; a little-wooded bottomland of gravel and boulders and sand and sheer rock islands, so spectacularly stratified that they looked like some giant child's laborious mudcakes—layer after laminated layer of red and brown and yellow and gray. Unimaginable torrents must have carved this canyon, in some distant age. The walls of it dwarfed the height of the islands—yet, clear to the top, the walls were nothing but strata.

Murno glanced at the strip of molten-gold sunlight along the eastern rim. "I'd like to get a look at the crossing while there's still light. Can we leave the horses here in cover and walk down?"

Wing shrugged. Parks said, "A couple of us will have to stay with them. Draw straws?"

There were nods. Parks got twigs. "Two shortest stay." As it happened, Parks himself got one of those. He shrugged, grinned at the clansman who shared his bad luck, and started leading the horses toward a stand of poplars.

112

The main canyon was a deeper, wider, more spectacular version of the tributary; with even less vegetation and more rock. The river was brisk and brown. The far wall, in dark shadow, looked solid. Murno peered along it. "The horses can wade those shallows downstream, but where do we get out on the other side?"

Wing said, "There's a tributary a few miles up, pretty much like this one we're in."

"All right," Murno said. He swept another look up and down stream. All looked peaceful. "Shall we get back to the horses? Maybe we can knock down a few rabbits for dinner."

They began retracing their steps. They hadn't gone more than a quarter of the way before a rifle-shot echoed down the canyon. After a frozen moment, Dal started up-canyon in a reckless run. Murno overtook him; tugged him near the wall. "Use your head! Whether they got away or not, we can't help them by running blind into an ambush!" He led the way more sensibly, dodging from cover to cover. But then there were four more shots in quick succession— and the scream of a horse.

Dal, on Murno's heels, said suddenly, "The saddle-bags!"

Shock lanced through Murno. The instruments! He'd left his pack hanging from the saddle! He reached for arrows as he ran. "Be careful! They may hover, waiting for the rest of us!"

It seemed to take forever to reach the spot, but eventually they crouched in cover, watching the canyon. The light was going now, but there were definitely no horses where they'd left them. "Stay here, but be ready!" Murno slipped from a willow patch; ran across the stream bent over, half expecting bullets to slam into him. He reached the poplars and saw deep hoofprints and sprays of dirt where the horses had sprinted hard up-canyon. He darted glances around; saw something farther back in the trees; ran to pick it up. His backpack, with the instruments in it! Obviously Parks or the other man had tossed it there before they mounted and broke up-canyon, leading all the horses.

But the rifle shots said they hadn't got far. And it wouldn't take the Gaddyl long to guess where the rest of

113

the party was. Suddenly he was shaking with rage. He fumbled at the pack; got out the handgun; set it for a narrow intense beam. Then he laid out his bow and four arrows handy. Finally he moved to where Dal and the others could see him, made handsigns to them to stay hidden, and stepped back out of sight.

When the aircar came slowly down the canyon, about forty feet above ground, with its canopy closed except for the small gun-ports, he watched it with no more compunction than if he were about to kill a rabbit for dinner.

First he put the energy-beam where it would fuse the drives, including the grav unit. Then—as the craft fell—he raked the beam along the canopy. Even before the car struck ground, aliens were screaming their death-agony. But one—the guide—must not be mortally hit, for the canopy flew open with a tearing sound and a rifle poked toward Murno. By that time he'd dropped the handgun and was nocking an arrow to save the handgun's energy. He might have been too slow with the arrow, but it didn't matter. Arrows from across the stream did the job.

He was at the aircar, making sure the aliens were all dead and that the radio wasn't on, when Dal and the others came running. Dal said, "I thought you said that handgun—"

Murno said woodenly, "In a canyon like this, they can't pinpoint it. Take what you want from this wreck, then go find Parks. I'll wait here. The Gaddyl can come if they want. I'm tired of running, for a while!"

One of the men growled, "Me too," but they all took weapons and radios and whatnot, then started upstream.

It was midnight before they'd buried the two men, wrestled the aircar to a rocky nook and piled stones over it, and dumped the Gaddyl corpses into the main river. By that time, all the horses except the one the Gaddyl had killed were rounded up.

Crossing the river, they saw no aircars. Neither was there any trouble in the small canyon they entered on the other side. By morning they were out of the tributary canyon and on a moderate elevation where they could study the way ahead. A few peaks showed above the horizon, but Murno knew those weren't the Rockies. That range was still out of sight.

As he rode, he felt absently of the instruments in his pack. The number of people who'd died to speed them along was mounting up. Whatever else happened now—assuming he himself didn't join the roster—he intended to deliver the damned things to "Omha," or erase that legend personally.

CHAPTER XIX: THE BURNIES

Pel—privileged, as a young acolyte, to watch the invocation—crouched in one of the Secret Places known to very few members of the tribe, peering through a very small hole in the hollowed-out rock. In the bare, sundrenched basin, his eldest uncle, Oggan, was donning the ancient robe of eagle-feathers, preparatory to the Autumn Invocation. Oggan's movements were slow and unsteady. He'd spent so many years in the Priesthood that the Emanations from Godstones had struck deeply into his marrow. His cheeks were hollow; his eyes shrunken and dim; his teeth all but gone; his skin covered with spots like bruises. Soon he would die; as had Pel's father, four summers past. Pel felt a rush of feeling. It was not right that so many of the tribe—more and more—withheld esteem from those who slowly perished of the Emanations. When Oggan was gone, the eagle-feather robe would fall to another of Pel's uncles, Jains The Surefooted, who as yet showed no sign of the Sickness. It would be many years before Pel could inherit the robe. He realized guiltily that he hadn't even been thinking of it lately—his mind and viscera were too full of his upcoming marriage to Wala, whom even old half-blind Oggan could see was the fairest of the tribe.

The shadow of the notched granite slab erected on the bare mountain behind Pel was creeping across the altar, a great upright block of the stone called Konn Kreet. Soon the shadow of the notch would fit the "V" etched on the altar. That happened only twice each year. Pel's lips moved silently with the ancient words of the Invocation, called "Prayer To Anatum." He shifted position to uncramp his legs—furtively; for the Gods must not be disturbed at the Holy Moment by an untoward sound.

Oggan stood up before the altar, his thin old arms outstretched to spread wide the robe. His voice came, cracked and quavering at first, then gaining depth and strength with the familiar intonation:

"Hear our prayer, O Lord Of Lightning
Who, wearied with the prideful past,
Did bludgeon down the great stone buildings
In rocking, rending, searing blast:

Spare our children from Thy sickness
(Old we are, and growing sere;
Younger hands must build Thy temples,
Bring Thee sacrificial deer):

Let Thy cunning guide our huntsmen:
Wither not our half-high grain:
Lend us Lesser-Fire-Spirit's
Warmth when winter comes again.

Harken to us, O Almighty
Whose wrath blew out what was before;
Whose unseen arrow guards the ruins;
Lord Of Lightning; God Of War."

Oggan let his arms drop tiredly. The last echo in the rocky basin died. Pel waited a minute, then got to hands and knees and crawled down the slanting tunnel by which he'd entered this Secret Place—carved, legend said, by the ancients during or just after the Gaddyl conquest—reached the exit, pushed up the cunningly-fitted slab, wormed out, closed the slab, and carefully replaced the rock-rubble that hid it. Then he hurried around to his uncle, who still stood, head down pensively, before the altar. "Come away, Uncle. No need to absorb more Emanation!" He stooped to pick up a small feather that had fallen from the robe.

"Thank you, youngster." Oggan took Pel's proffered arm and let himself be helped toward the twisting cleft that led out of the basin. "If Omha would give just a small sign . . . I've waited so many years, and now I have few left."

Pel said emphatically, "He does give signs! Does he not send the rain and the sun, that crops may thrive and game

116

be plentiful? Does he not permit Godstones to continue Emanating, to protect us from enemies? Does the tribe not flourish?"

Oggan paused in his painful walking to catch his breath. "Yes," he said listlessly, "the tribe flourishes. Or it has, until this new trouble with the aliens. But the least faithful flourish best of all. It is we who serve, who sacrifice our bodies and our years, who do not flourish. And now Omha permits the aliens to hunt us just as cruelly as they hunt the Orse or other infidels. Why?"

Pel, stomach tightening with anxiety, stared at his uncle. This near-heresy, from the Priest of Priests? "Perhaps," he muttered, "it is precisely because we seem to grow less faithful. Perhaps the huntsmen who were killed were guilty of heresy or of overweaning pride. Uncle, you're not beginning to doubt, are you? We *know* that Omha exists!"

Oggan nodded tiredly. "Yes, nephew. There are the Miraculous Happenings. What I am doubting is not His existence. My discontent is that I am beginning to see that we may be wrong in expecting from Him such mundane virtues as gratitude toward individuals. We are as ants, and He is a God. His purposes are not our purposes. His comprehension is not our comprehension."

Pel, profoundly disturbed, said, "If you have not gotten your reward in this life, Uncle, you'll get it in the next."

Oggan grinned with a touch of his old humor, revealing the discolored remnants of his teeth. "I'll soon enough find out. Don't let my mood depress you, youngster—I lived my life fiercely and joyously when I was able, and you must live yours that way." He paused. "Be especially careful when you go on Sentry watch tomorrow. There's no knowing whether the Gaddyl may follow some of our huntsmen home. Or whether Orse may try to take refuge in the mountains. That could bring disaster upon us. Watch carefully, that no one stumbles into the secret approaches."

"I shall, Uncle." Pel swept a last scrutiny around the basin, making sure that no blades of grass were sprouting in any of the carefully-laid-out but unmarked paths. Most of the basin, of course, was kept carefully sterile by the Godstones his ancestors had collected from various ruins and brought here—and, indeed, no plant or animal could live long anywhere in the basin—but occasionally some

117

bird flying over would drop a seed or two. Strangers, including Gaddyl in aircars, who happened this way might wonder how a grass-shoot could be alive in an area obviously cursed with Emanations.

The paths were clean. He led Oggan around a cluster of Godstones that looked as if they'd just happened to tumble there (he knew every Emanating stone in the place, of course; could have threaded the safest way among them with his eyes shut) and headed for the cleft. "After my honeymoon, Uncle, I'll lead a crew to drag some more Godstones from the nearest ruins. If the Gaddyl are going to be hunting Wild Folk, we'll want a wider area sterilized."

The sky was barely lightening when Pel shrugged into shoulder-straps, took his bow in his left hand, and left the sentries' breakfast-circle. Someone called after him, "Don't sit on a Godstone, Bridegroom-to-be!" There was a burst of laughter at the threadbare joke. He felt his cheeks redden. There was always speculation among the uninitiated, as to whether a priest-acolyte might not already have exposed his loins to too much Emanation. Pel knew he hadn't.

He went westward, down the ravine kept carefully clear of vegetation (and furnished with enough weak Emanation to register on Gaddyl instruments, should the aliens for some reason put on breathing-apparatus and land this high in the mountains). He paused to scuff out with his moccasins a set of deer-tracks from the night before. Someone, he thought, would have to hunt down that cougar that frightened deer into this barren ravine.

At the mouth of the ravine he paused to survey the canyon it emptied into. There was a convincing sparsity of vegetation just below the ravine; Emanation washed down by rains. He walked on hurriedly to minimize his own exposure.

Two thousand feet or more he descended; turned westward again onto the brow of a cliff; settled himself in the familiar sentry-spot beneath a stunted pine forced to grow low and spreading by the steady south wind. He squirmed out of the packstraps; unbuttoned the deerskin pack and got out his waterbag; untied the corner and took

118

a long drink. The last time he'd done Sentry here, the time had passed quickly—he'd been wrapped in his dreams about Wala. Today, there were less pleasant things on his mind.

His own people—Burnies, as the Orse called them—could adapt to the new viciousness of the Gaddyl. There was no need to go down to low altitudes in the daytime. Grain could be gathered, deer could be hunted, at night. And the Emanation had always been a good defense for his people in their high retreats. But why did Omha allow the aliens to prey upon Wild Folk at all? There was no doctrine saying that the Orse, for instance, were beyond the benevolence of Omha.

Could it be that Omha was unwilling to move against the aliens because that would reveal his existence? Doctrine was unclear on the relationship of Omha to the Gaddyl. Doctrine just said that some day Omha would smite the aliens, and that men would once more own their planet. In the meantime, was Omha not strong enough to protect humans? No one claimed that He was omnipotent, or that He was the only God.

Maybe the aliens had a stronger God, who protected them for the moment. The thought was disturbing. In fact, the whole chain of thought was disturbing—it made Pel realize that he'd never thought of Omha except as a local force—that, actually, his thinking was very vague where the rest of the world was concerned. He wished he were near an altar, so he might make a prayer for guidance.

He twisted into a more comfortable position and stared out over the slopes below him. It was going to be a long day. There was a herd of bison far out on the plain—a mere smudge—but no sign of either Orse or Gaddyl hunting them. To the south, a few wispy clouds drifted; not enough to bring rain. He turned his attention to the slopes, nearer. A flock of white goats were grazing on a sparse flat near the creek that twisted down westward from his left. Vultures, circling a little way beyond, probably meant that something had killed a goat last night and was still guarding the carcass.

It was an hour before noon when he caught a glimpse of mounted men coming up the creek.

Anxiously, Pel watched the places along the stream where he'd be able to see the horsemen. Presently they filed into sight—first, the middle-aged clean-shaven man wearing a sheepskin jacket, and seated upon the black bison-skin saddle of the local Orse. Then a beared man a little older, with a leather garment unlike any Pel had ever seen; with heavy heeled boots; wearing at his belt both a knife and a handgun of some kind. His bow, slung across his back, was wooden and unusually long. Then six other men in assorted garments. All their bows were wooden too, shorter than the bearded man's, but certainly not local weapons—all the Orse Pel knew of carved their bows from the long horns of a certain kind of cattle.

Clearly, this was no simple band of refugees fleeing into the mountains!

Foliage intervened. When he could see them again, Pel noted other things: the bearded man did not sit his horse as easily as the others, but his eyes, roving the ravine ahead, knew just where to look. This was no man of the Orse—he was a woodsman. And—Pel saw now—the holstered handgun was Gaddyl; the small object on a thong around the stranger's neck, no amulet, but a Gaddyl radio!

It was obvious from the way the men kept to cover, and turned wary looks to the sky, that they feared the Gaddyl. The horses—there were two extra, bearing only packs—were gaunt and weary.

Pel's pulse quickened. Strangers—enemies of the Gaddyl—arriving the very next day after the Autumn Invocation! Could this be the sign old Oggan yearned for?

But caution restrained him. Equally, the strangers might bring the trouble Oggan feared.

He watched the slow progress of the group. When the shoulder of the cliff hid them, he did not run to where he could see them again, but withdrew eastward. He wanted to be at a certain spot where he could watch them as they neared the barren ravine down which he'd come. Depending on how they acted, his duty would be either to meet them and misdirect them, or to run up to Sentry headquarters and warn of their coming.

The sun beat down almost vertically into the canyon. Pel, on the western slope, peered through foliage at the

120

steadily-climbing horsemen. They kept the watch on the sky, of course, but they were making no effort to hide themselves otherwise. They weren't even holding their voices down; the talk drifted faintly up to him. And they didn't seem nervous—only the local Orse, who very probably had in the past exchanged threats if not arrows with Pel's people, showed any worry. The bearded man was merely alert. The rest were plainly curious about the country, and not at home in it.

The local Orse reined in, glanced around nervously, and said something to the bearded man. That individual sat his horse silently for a minute. Then—shockingly—he looked almost straight toward Pel's hiding place, held out his hands to show they were empty, and called out calmly, "We're looking for you. We're friends."

Pel crouched motionless, bewildered. A Sentry's directives didn't cover this!

Common sense, though, demanded that he find out what the strangers wanted. Slowly, he straightened, stepped clear of cover and showed his empty hands as the bearded man had and then began descending the slope. When he was close he asked the bearded man a little petulantly, "How did you locate me?"

"The birds were avoiding that spot. Are you one of the people called Burnies?"

Pel put aside mild resentment. "Yes. What do you want of us?"

The stranger watched him silently for a moment. "I have an errand I may need your help with. These others just want to cross the mountains to talk alliance with Orse clans beyond. We're all enemies of the Gaddyl."

Pel said doubtfully, "I don't know that we can help you. There's no good pass through here—twenty miles south is the nearest. And the country here isn't hospitable. I just happen to be here, seeking higher hunting territory. With the Gaddyl acting as they are—"

The local Orse said, a trifle pugnaciously, "I know your tribe lives even higher than this! And I know there are ways through the mountains!"

The bearded man put out a hand to restrain the Orse. "What about that pass you mentioned? Could my friends reach it from here without going back down too far?"

Pel saw a way out. "They can. Two miles down, there's a fork of this creek that leads south. You must have passed it. If they'll follow up that, they'll find the headwaters in a blind canyon. It won't be too hard to climb around the mountain that blocks them—either flank is all right—and from its eastern slope they'll be able to see a way east. But I'd advise you to stay with them. These mountains, at night. . . ."

The bearded man said, "I have to visit your tribe, at least for a parley." He turned to the others. "Why don't you scout the way? If I'm coming after you, I'll be at that mountain he describes by tomorrow night. If I'm not there, move on." He dismounted; removed a pack from the saddle; handed the reins to the local Orse. "If I turn back west, I'll find a horse somewhere lower down. Thanks for everything. Maybe we'll meet again."

The others were silent and a little glum. One—a young man with light eyes—reined his horse around so he could reach down a hand. "I hope so, Murno. We've been through quite a lot together. I hope you find your family safe. If you want to bring them to Larkan's clan, they'll be welcome."

The bearded man smiled grimly. "Thanks." He shook hands all around. "I wouldn't bet much on the chances, but if I can, I'll look you up."

Pel waited nervously until the farewells ended and the horses were filing down-canyon. Now, he thought, there was only the man called Murno to deal with. But whether to take him to the tribe, as he asked . . .

The man looked at him for a moment with a faint smile—and with a hint of some strong emotion—then said suddenly, "Omha Abides!"

Pel went rigid with astonishment. Then, his heart beginning to thump, he said shakily, "You . . . a foreigner . . . a Believer?" He looked hastily down-canyon to make sure the Orse were gone. "I must take you to my uncle!"

Pel lay on his sleeping-pad, mind churning. Never in his life had he felt so miserable. How could his uncles Oggan and Jains be so blind? How could they so doubt Omha's will? If it were not Omha's will, how could the stranger Murno have come to this very spot—across such tremendous stretches of land, under the noses of the Gaddyl, miraculously escaping such an array of perils?

But his uncles did doubt. Simply because one of the two instruments Murno offered was clearly Gaddyl, while the other seemed to be an artifact of the ancients; the sinful, overweening humans who'd ruled Earth before the Conquest.

If Omha were any kind of a God (which Pel did not doubt!) Omha could certainly deal with two small contrivances, whether they be Gaddyl or ancient. To Pel, it was clear and simple. Omha was not, perhaps, omnipotent, but He could do certain things. And He had motivated Murno to bring the artifacts here, and guided and protected Murno—because *Omha wanted the artifacts.* It made no difference that Murno was not, as Pel had at first assumed, a true Believer.

Yet Oggan and Jains and such other elders of the tribe as were privy to the momentous arrival argued and pondered, saying that such artifacts were in no way part of Omha's dominion, and might be some devilish trick of the Gaddyl.

What awful things, Pel thought miserably, might befall if the artifacts Omha wanted were withheld by his own Priesthood? He groaned and rolled over, trying to find at least some physical comfort. This evening, he should have been with Wala in her father's tree-bower, discussing honeymoon plans. Instead, he'd been locked in bitter argument with the elders. He hoped Wala could understand.

But, at least Murno had been shrewd. Watchful—and not above exploiting the elders' uncertainty—he'd kept the two instruments; had chosen his own sleeping-spot where, should trouble come, the Gaddyl handgun would outweigh a hundred arrows.

Suddenly, Pel's misery was too much. He cast off his blanket and rolled to his feet. He crouched for a moment listening to the snores of the other young men. He reached for his belt, bow and quiver; felt with his toes for his moccasins and wiggled his feet into them. At the screen of boulders that sheltered this sleeping-place he paused and peered around at the starlit slope before starting down.

As he expected, the bearded man was awake, and heard

him coming. "Murno! It's me!" He was aware of the Gaddyl handgun aimed at him. "I cannot agree with my uncles. Bring your artifacts. I will take you to an altar so you can offer them to Omha!"

The basin was eerie by starlight. Pel held his voice to a whisper, though there was no sleeping-place nor Sentry post within half a mile. "Follow behind me. There is Emanation, but if you avoid the sources it will not harm you in the short time we are here." He led the circuitous way until they were facing the altar-stone; hesitated uncertainly. An acolyte was not fit to make an invocation —and what of Murno, standing in plain sight? He muttered, "Let Omha judge," took a deep breath and intoned, "Great Omha, Protector and Mentor, forgive our unworthiness. A stranger has brought two artifacts: this is he, and he holds them in his hands. In his own way, he believes —and I in full faith believe—that You caused them to be brought here. Will you claim them now?"

He stood a moment, roiling with uncertainty. Would there perhaps have to a special kind of invocation; a particular time of night or day? Or—maybe he and Murno must lay the artifacts before the altar and withdraw. He turned his head toward the bearded man; opened his mouth to speak . . .

A faint movement of air impinged on his skin, not scented, exactly, but warm and . . . different . . . as if some great beast had exhaled toward him. His heart contracted with panic. He tensed—felt his muscles go lax again, with no intent of his—saw Murno stagger two steps, still clutching the instruments. He realized with astonishment that he himself was about to fall. He lurched toward Murno. "Over there! We must get away from the . . ."

But his voice failed as his legs were failing, and he slumped, powerless, beside the bearded man—directly before the altar stone, where Emanations were worst! He squirmed, groaned once, and lost consciousness.

The sun, just clearing the east rim of the basin, was warm on his face. That was Pel's first waking sensation. His first coherent thought was that he—and perhaps

Murno—had lain the night through in deadly Emanation.

He rolled over and scrambled to his feet, then went rigid. He was not near the altar! Instead, he was across the basin, in a spot where the Emanation was minimal. Murno lay there too, face up, slack-mouthed, looking in sleep old and tired. Murno's backpack, bow and quiver lay neatly placed beside him.

But the two artifacts were gone.

Pel almost shouted for joy. A Miraculous Happening! Omha had heard! He bent; shook the sleeping man. "Murno! Murno! We were right!"

The limp body stirred and the eyes opened heavily. A moment and life leaped into them. Murno came to his feet like a cat; reached to seize Pel's jacket. "You sneaking fraud!"

Pel, bewildered, tried to pull free, but Murno's grasp was too strong. "Wha—what—" Comprehension came. He quit trying to escape. "You think I tricked you? You think this was a scheme to get the artifacts away from you, and that I—" Anger flooded over him. "You are no Believer at all!" He pointed suddenly at Murno's bow on the ground. "Must I supply the faith for all? Release me, Doubter! There is your bow. I will stand with my face against the altar-stone. Fill my back with arrows, if you can!"

The bearded man stared into his eyes; slowly relaxed the grip on his jacket. Pel strode toward the altar. "Wait!" the older man said harshly. Pel ignored him and walked on. An arrow whicked past his ear and slammed against the stone. He laughed. "See? You cannot hit me!" He glanced back in derision. Murno was watching him intently. He reached the stone; stood with his nose almost touching it.

Murno said, "You'd better not move a muscle, fellow." An arrow barely grazed Pel's right shoulder. Then another grazed his left. A third tugged at his hair, directly over the crown of his skull—but did not crease his scalp! He flinched as chips of the konn kreet stung his forehead.

Murno said, "Turn around."

Pel complied, a little uncertainly. Murno had another arrow half-drawn. But the older man slowly relaxed the bowstring, let go with his right hand, and drew the Gaddyl weapon. "With this, I can fry you against that thing you

125

call an altar—and vaporize the altar too. But the energy-burst might bring Gaddyl. Is your faith that strong?"

Fear lanced into Pel. He leaped hastily away from the altar-stone. "No! Not—not the alien weapon! Kill me with an arrow; but do not bring—" Slowly he went limp; gazed at the bearded man almost tearfully. "Stranger, I—I am not sure Omha is stronger than the Gaddyl!"

Murno, face unreadable, eyed him steadily. "Who took the instruments?"

"Omha! I—I swear it!"

Murno smiled briefly and grimly. "What did he look like?"

"I did not see, of course! I was put to sleep, as you were! We fell near the—Omha moved us, stranger, to where the Emanation would not harm us!"

"Did you feel yourself being moved?"

"No."

"Then," Murno said, "how do you know someone—men of your tribe—didn't come here, take the instruments, and move us?"

"I . . ." Pel's gaze dropped. How could he convince this stranger, when the Worm of Doubt was gnawing at his own entrails? He looked around desperately. "They would not come to this holy place. You, stranger—infidel—if you did not believe in Omha, why did you bring the artifacts?"

Murno's face showed a mishmash of emotions. Slowly, he holstered the handgun. "That's a very good question, young man. I took a vow when I was about your age, but. . . . And why have all the others—men you've never heard of, whose ways of life you can't conceive—helped me? Hope, I guess. We all hoped there was something in the legend. Tell me straight—if you believe Omha took the instruments and moved us to safer places, how did he do it?"

"Why—it was a Miraculous Happening! There have been many—doctrine records them!" Pel turned suddenly and ran to the spot where gravel covered the trapdoor he'd used two days before. He kicked the rubble aside. "This basin is an ancient Holy Place. See—here is a tunnel! My people could hardly cut, thus, through solid rock. This slab that covers the hole—"

Murno was beside him, eagerly. "Where does it lead?"

126

"Only to a secret observation-place. My great-grand-father found this one. There are others. Some, perhaps, that we do not know of."

The bearded man was running his fingers along the edge of the thin slab. "This is not natural stone!"

"Perhaps not. Doctrine does not mention these places. We believe that the ancients made them; that they too worshipped Omha . . ." He stood up as Murno did. "Why will you not believe me? I've sinned against my own Priesthood—defied my uncles and my elders—to help you bring the artifacts here!"

Murno was replacing the slab. "I do not believe you because I *must* not. Yet I don't entirely disbelieve you, either. Here—rearrange this gravel to suit yourself, and let's get moving. If you're telling the truth, you don't want your tribe to find you here!"

Pel started to say that Omha would protect him, but stopped. Maybe—as Oggan suggested—Omha was too busy to watch over every individual every moment. Murno's arrows had flown disconcertingly true. And their hammered-iron points had marred the altar-stone, with no sign of anger from Omha.

They were through the cleft and a couple of hundred yards away when a soft call came from behind a boulder. Oggan hobbled into sight, straining under a burden—Pel's backpack. "I guessed what you'd done, Nephew. I've brought your things and some food. You must be away quickly—the judgment will be death, if you're caught." His old eyes fixed on Murno. "Stranger, will you be a friend to my nephew?"

"Yes."

Pel, achurn with feelings, hesitated. "But—my marriage!"

"It's impossible now. I'll explain to Wala. Go, Nephew! Hurry!" Then Oggan half-raised a hand. "But, one thing—what happened in the basin?"

"Omha gave us sleep! And took the artifacts!"

Oggan smiled. "Thank you, nephew. It will be interesting to see whether I can eventually convince the tribe. Farewell."

Pel stood a moment watching the old man hobble away, then turned to Murno. "We must take a difficult path, to evade pursuit. Perhaps you will tolerate my company on your trip westward." His voice, surprisingly, was quite steady. But inside him was a terrible aching hollowness.

CHAPTER XX: THE JUDGEMENT OF OMHA

—RM 1297 64 3493.89173 TS SCR ATT OM AKN.
—OM 4106 518 3493.89186 AKN RM GA.
—RM WL SN FAC RGS 2 INST JS AQ 1 GAD 1 RS.
—OM STG B GA.

One Point One, Omaha Command Center, came awake with a surging of currents and a clicking of relays. His consciousness did not all turn on at once—when he was already awake enough to think coherently, components were still plugging in. He felt a touch of the feedback corresponding to annoyance. It was definitely not proper procedure to bring him to awareness before he was plugged in to all the memory-banks and sensors he was supposed to have. He himself activated one of the latter; scanned a lightless grotto far below the topsoil; demanded gratingly via an audio-grill, "Why are you repairbots not activated?"

One of the octopus-like metal things stirred. "Most of us are on Minimum Survival to conserve energy."

One Point One shot a query to Chrono; learned that the year was 3493. "Good Heavens," a personality-component whispered somewhere, ghostlike. One Point One felt the tiny DC pulsations that corresponded to amusement. Six hundred years of sleep might seem long to a Human-Personality-Residue. To One Point One, it was just another statistic. He tested out his sensors (including many innovations that had not been devised by his original builders), letting Monitor—it was One Point Seven on duty, he noted—wait. A little anxiety-feedback, he thought, might teach One Point Seven not to jerk his superior so rudely out of sleep. "Repairbots: Directly under my Section J-29 is some earthquake damage."

"We are aware of it. Temporary shoring was installed fifty-three years ago."

"Well, get at it and make a nice smooth patch on the concrete, and pump high-density grout into the cavity. Energy expenditure is authorized."

"We will do it at once."

Deliberately, One Point One let his attention drift back to Monitor. "Now, Impatient One. What is it?"

Monitor said relievedly, "There is an important matter, though not an emergency. I thought it best not to feed it to you until you'd had a chance to adjust to being awake again."

"So; I'm adjusted." One Point One allowed himself a smug moment. His subordinates treated him with more awe than the chain of command actually required. They were only machines; estimable in their abilities, but machines. He—with his array of Personality-Transcriptions—was undoubtedly a little more.

He let Monitor's information flow into him. After a few milliseconds he abruptly went into high gear. Relays clacked; lights flashed on in a dozen deep caverns that had lain dark for centuries. Special personality-banks hummed with test currents; joined the network; seemed to whisper in a chorus of querulous voices.

"Full Alert!" One Point One snapped, "Full Conference!"

He waited, suppressing feedback, while a myriad of tiny spiderbots swarmed about long-unused banks, testing, replacing a few components that had gone dead. Though he did not apologize to Monitor, he admitted to himself that Monitor had used good judgment. This thing would have been far too ampere-producing to foist upon him fresh from slumber and unadjusted.

It was minutes before everybody tested GO. Then he activated circuits to cut in various voice-boxes. A warning-current suddenly circled in his interior: the audio-system must be retested to make sure no sound could carry to the surface nor into any new rock-faults or newly-drilled wells. Five more minutes. Finally the warning-current ceased.

"This is One Point One." His mechanical voice echoed in more than sixty local chambers, deep in bedrock. "I am conducting this conference in audible English because many Personality-Transcripts will participate, and we are conscious of the effects of semantics." He paused. "The following have just been acquired by Rocky Mountain outpost: one Mark 17 DB Scanner which is almost certainly the one which—as Monitor has noted in General Memory-log—had apparently fallen into alien hands. And one Gaddyl device, obviously capable of being fed high amperage, which is very probably a small version of the Distorter."

An utter chaos of currents assaulted One Point One. He damped them to bearability; hushed, for a moment, the audio-speakers. "Gentlemen, gentlemen! And lady. Please! One at a time. General M, you are senior."

A slightly raspy, emotion-keyed voice whispered, "I have no vote since I am not a PT but only a mock-up after death. But I say, throw every erg of our technological resources into an immediate study. Spare no expenditure! Master this Distorter—probe every secret that lurks in it! Then equip our missiles to counteract it, and attack! Attack! Attack!"

One Point One suppressed a sigh. "Thank you, General M. General E?

This was a full PT, and contained far more of the donor's actual personality. "Well, certainly we should begin the study, not neglecting, of course, all necessary safeguards. But we should do nothing hasty. Would an all-out study jeopardize our security?"

One Point One said, "The earlier stages carry no danger. Later, possibly, if empirical tests become necessary, we would have to compute the risks."

General E's circuits hummed for a few milliseconds. "Can an estimate be made now of the probable elapsed time of the study? And of the energy-and-materials expenditure?"

One Point One, of course, had already considered those things. "Probable study time cannot be estimated until we have some grasp of the Distorter's nature. Absolute minimum would be eighty hours. Possible maximum, infinity. So far as energy and materials go, I've estimated those as equal to one-twentieth our regular expenditure for maintenance. There is no worry there."

General E asked, "Assuming we could solve and

duplicate the Distorter quickly, or build some counter-measure, do we have a significant number of operative missiles left and would there be any difficulty in modifying them? And are they suitably dispersed?"

"There has been," One Point One said, "no significant change since the most recent survey fed into your memory-banks. That is, we are within ninety per cent of the readiness we had just following the capitulation of Earth."

There was a murmur from the female Transcript. "Yes, Madam L," One Point One said, "full expenditure of our warheads would certainly cause widespread death and suffering." He recognized another voice. "General O?"

General O seldom concerned himself with tactics. "There is still a question in my mind regarding the matter of possible enemy reinforcement. At the time of the conquest, there were forty-three known Translocation Centers in orbit around Sol. We know that some of those were shifted elsewhere after the Gaddyl victory. Do we know whether any remain at this moment? And how many Centers have they on Earth now? The last estimate I have is minimum, one; maximum, one thousand. Can't we do better than that?"

"We can. We even have a probability figure now: point nine nine two that all the attack centers were sent elsewhere. And a probable number of centers now on Earth: one point six three."

General O snorted. "Does that mean they have one, or do they have two?"

One Point One felt amusement-feedback. "You may have your choice, General. We know of one, in what used to be the State of Arizona. Unfortunately we have no sensors overseas, and it has long been policy not to send spy-apparatus via air or water. We only speculate that, for logistic reasons, they might have another at the antipodes. That speculation is reflected in the figure I quote."

General O said with deep irony, "Thank you very much."

A Transcript designated "Admiral J" put in, "This is out of my line, of course, but have any active human troop units been found? My last datum on that is negative."

"There has been," One Point One answered impatiently, "no detected human action against the Gaddyl that can be

131

classed as resistance or rebellion. There are constantly incidents, of course, but these must be considered civil crimes. About fifty years after the conquest, the last group of United States infantrymen ambushed a small squad of Gaddyl security troops and killed them. They themselves were overtaken and destroyed within an hour. All of them, of course, were old men. No, Admiral, there is no organized resistance. The children don't even play soldier any more. Or sailor."

There were more questions, and more opinions. But before long it became clear that (aside from the personality-mock-up of General M) there was no significant will. And there were no ideas worth analysis.

One Point One let them think the discussion was continuing, but gradually, regretfully, gently, he damped out the emotions in them; put them back to sleep; probed into their memory-banks and excised all recollection of this conference. It could all be fed back, of course, if that became advisable—but meanwhile they must be restored to their pristine conditions, lest, under the impact of this new experience and information, their personalities change.

Before he turned off the last audio speakers, a sound very much like a sigh came through. It was his own sigh. The results of such a conference were always predictable. And even if, sometime, some definite will, some purpose— such as General M might show—were to emerge, he, on analysis, would probably have to override it. He held the conferences because he was basically programmed to do so—his long-dead builders had done what they could to assure human, not machine, decisions. But he always hoped. Each time, there was a trickle of anxiety-feedback in him, a hope—that was the only word for it—that the taped human personalities would this time come up with a—well, with an "inspiration."

That hopeful feeling, he guessed, could be blamed on whatever of him was other-than-machine.

Now, he let that part of him seek its own lurking-circuits while he addressed his purely electronic-and-mechanical subordinates: "To a high probability, the device we are now studying is a Distorter. To a fair probability, we can solve it quickly. To a fair probability, we could modify

132

most of our operative missiles to counteract the enemy defense.

"The regaining of our own spy device is of course fortunate, but that in itself is reason to reassess our security. We can not rely on fortune. Obviously, we have been indiscreet—that is, we have miscalculated the risks.

"Beginning at once, but with utmost caution, we will withdraw a large part of our sensory apparatus from the surface. Especially near Gaddyl habitations and installations, we will cease, for the time, all spying.

"Precisely because we have this extremely important device to study, we must be careful. Short-range objectives such as watching the situation on the surface must be subordinated to security.

"I wish to state this another way, for my own benefit: the present suffering of humans must not lead us risk in any way our long-range objective, which is the eventual retaking of the planet. If humans are hunted for a generation, two generations, ten—if the race is reduced to the status of jungle beasts—that is not important! So long as breeding-stock remains, the race can regenerate."

Before he broke the circuits, he made a little joke which he knew would not be understood: "We are going underground."

CHAPTER XXI: INVITATION TO FOLLY

Murno sat bundled in a bison-hide blanket, his back against a pine-trunk, and stared pensively down the rocky open slope toward a small creek. The slope looked no less harsh by moonlight. On the way east, he recalled, he'd thought this a singularly unattractive spot. Now, he appreciated it—Gaddyl wouldn't come here.

The dozen and more men snoring behind him, under the few scraggily trees, were Orse from various clans between the Rockies and this lesser range. Not one of them had ever been this far west, which made him the guide. He grinned to himself at the thought. How long was it since he'd led someone named Klayr, and three youngsters, out of a fertile valley just over a ridge from a Fiefdom? Two months? He realized with sudden horror that he could no longer visualize Klayr clearly. When he tried, other things got in the way—the faces of Gaddyl he'd killed, of men who'd been killed at his side.

The Gaddyl radio he carried was murmuring something. He snuggled it against his ear; heard a guide somewhere reporting a campfire. Let them swoop down on it—they'd find no Wild Folk around it, unless those were bait. Free humans were becoming wary game.

One of the tethered horses whickered softly. He heard Pel speak to it quietly. The young Burnie had certainly become a good man, and fast. Not the most cheerful company, but reliable.

The horse whickered again, louder. This time, an answering whinny came from the thicket along the creek. Murno threw off the robe, felt about for his bow and for the Gaddyl rifle he carried nowadays. He saw Pel step into the moonlight and walk slowly down-slope. That was correct; to show himself while the rest of the group remained hidden. He heard the men behind him tossing off their blankets and getting to their feet. One of them went to the horses.

A mounted man left the creek and rode slowly to meet Pel. There was a brief conversation, then Pel turned and called out, "They're scouts. Their clan-leader's name is Sander."

Murno called, "Bring them up. I know the clan."

Four horsemen altogether rode up; dismounted at his invitation. "He said, "Aren't you scouting a little out of your territory? I thought your clan was settled farther north."

The spokesman said, "We're combining rounds with eight or nine other clans now. We're on the watch for anyone travelling west."

Murno asked, "Why?"

"Because a top man called Larkan wants to see them."

Larkan—with the beginning of a beard, and looking gaunter and older—eyed Murno. "So you made it. What became of my men?"

"Parks and one other got killed. Dal and the rest went on east of the Rockies. From what we heard, they could go a long way and not run out of clans."

Larkan grunted. "I hope they didn't try. Murno, I've learned one thing—it's nonsense to think about co-ordinating defense over any distance. We just can't communicate fast enough. Not long after you left, a party of twelve Gaddyl killed fourteen people of a clan north of us, then camped at a small lake. I had a messenger there to offer an alliance, and he joined an attack on the Gaddyl camp. He got himself killed, which demonstrated his sincerity. But it was four days before we even got the word!"

Murno nodded. "Any combined attack would have to be planned ahead, and it would have to be against a fixed target. About all we can do is exchange whatever information we can; share ideas and tactics. And maybe food and shelter when they're needed." He stared idly toward the horses, tethered among the pines, feeding hungrily on grass that had been cut and brought to them. "I've been thinking, more or less vaguely. . . . After I make sure my family's safe, I may try to organize a roving band to hit the Gaddyl wherever they hunt too enthusiastical-ly." He paused for a minute. "I haven't talked much about some of the mutants I've met, but they've got abilities you and I can't match. The Big Ears, for instance—I think they could see clearly by starlight alone. And even when they can't see, they can hear things a cat can't."

Larkan said, "I'm way ahead of you. We've got over four dozen of them with us as refugees, and I've persuaded some of them to ride horses. A few nights ago a couple went out with us on a deer hunt. They can sneak right up on a deer in the dark and touch it! The trouble is, they won't kill anything. They have to be practically starved before they'll even eat meat!"

Murno said, "Refugees?"

Larkan nodded grimly. "The whole north half of the Grove is gone. The Gaddyl cut a line across the middle, then started a slow drive, burning as they went. There was an awful smoke and an awful stink for days. The Grove didn't burn very well, and they were using heavy beamers." Larkan sat silent for a minute, right hand idly fingering a Gaddyl rifle across his lap. "You should have seen the mess of day-blind animals and Big Ears that came out! In the

135

daytime, they could only stumble around blindly. The only reason anything got away was, there was just plain more than the Gaddyl could kill."

Murno watched the clan leader's face. Dare he ask if there'd been any blue-skinned mutants among the victims? He'd better not, yet. There was always the chance that the Gaddyl might capture and interrogate someone who'd heard a bit of gossip. Instead, he told Larkan, "The heavy beamers are just one of the things they can use against us if they have to. There's a lot of stuff you've never seen."

Larkan said, "No, but you have, and you can tell us what to expect. Look, Murno—I'm not stupid enough to think we can fight them with bows and arrows and the few guns we've already got. But, say they turn heavier stuff against us—those beamers, for instance. If I'd had a day or so to plan and prepare, I could have had an ambush ready in the Grove! We could have jumped them and grabbed some of those beamers! And with enough men, I could have overwhelmed them!" He leaned forward excitedly. "Stay with me, Murno! With your knowledge we can take them in a dozen ambushes! We can make ourselves into an army, with real weapons!"

For a moment, Larkan's intensity swept Murno along. Then the intoxication passed. He said patiently, "You're aiming at the wrong part of the animal. By making the hunting more difficult and more costly for the guests, you can minimize it. But what you're talking about would be suicide. Suppose, just for instance, you could seize a real array of weapons—do you know what they'd do? They'd just bring in a few fighting-ships from off-planet. You've seen the ruins. Can't you tell from them how the ancients must have fought? They had technology of their own, and real weapons. But they were crushed!"

For a moment Larkan's eyes blazed at Murno as if *he* were the enemy. Then the Orse leader grinned coldly. "They couldn't bring in any fighting ships, though, could they, if we knocked out Ingress before they knew what was happening?" He got to his feet. "You're bound and determined to go look after your family, and I can't blame you for that. But promise me one thing—that as soon as you can, you'll come back. I won't do anything in the meantime to spill the stew, but I'll be making preparations. And you be thinking!"

Murno, a little dazed, stared at him. Finally he said, "All right, Larkan. I'll come back if I can, and I'll be thinking. But I don't think my opinion will change."

CHAPTER XXII: OORY GOES FISHING

Oory let his small aircar settle to the surface of the bay; sat listening to the familiar "slap-slap-slap" of small waves against the hull. He slid back the canopy. The bay was sparkling-blue, clean, inviting. But he wasn't here to swim.

He watched the aircars shooting southward along the Coast Flyway. Presently one dipped and swerved to come toward this restricted patch of water. It rocked once laterally as a signal, slanted down toward him, and settled lightly to the water. Its canopy slid open and Oj Liave grinned in pleasure. "Eminence!"

Oory said a trifle severely, "You know very well that's no longer my title! But I exult at seeing you again. Did you have any trouble avoiding questions?"

"None worth remembering. Guddun is away touring other Fiefdoms—he's trying to get agreement on lower indemnities to guests hunting Wild Folk. I think he'll get it, too. You should see the waiting lists!"

Oory said grimly, "I've seen the actual hunting. A slaughter, and not entirely one-sided. There've been times when I've almost been glad of that. When bloodthirsty nincompoops pump bullets into women and children. . . . But I have not told you my reason for coming. I was allowed to read your report of the raid on the Bluies."

Oj Liave's eyes membraned over for an instant. "I did not enjoy that. Guddun insisted."

"No doubt," Oory said. "Old Friend, I am going to burden you with a barbed secret. My particular job is not merely, as publicly announced, the pursuit of notorious Wild Folk. Confidentially, Stolm has a very hot fish in his hands—the loss of a Distorter. I will be the Offering, of course, if the word gets out. But Stolm will not be smothered in garlands, either, so he hopes to recover the thing and hush up the whole affair. *That* is my real job. And I need your help."

Oj Liave nictated politely. "You know I will help in any way possible."

Oory grinned. "That is what I rely on. You are aware that our old friend Murno has now become a badly wanted fugitive. I have strong reason to believe that his family was with the Blue Mutants. I was disappointed to note that they were not among the prisoners you took, but I am almost certain they were with the mutants who escaped to the north. I see, furthermore, that one young Normal was taken in the raid—a former neighbor of Murno."

"That is right, Old Friend."

"Murno," Oory went on, "is somewhere far to the east, and trying to find him is like looking for a minnow in a tule marsh. I had hoped to use his family as bait to draw him out of the marsh. However—" Oory paused and studied the Elder Patron's face, "if Murno can be made to *believe* that we have his family, that may serve quite as well."

Oj Liave eyed him with a certain wariness. "But if he is far to the east and out of touch, how will he even know about the raid?"

Oory said, "We can arrange to let him know. I want you to allow a few of those prisoners to escape."

Oj Liave looked as if he'd swallowed something he hadn't intended to. "Did I hear you right? Guddun has ordered us emphatically to take the greatest care with these prisoners. After interrogating them, he intends, if he finds them innocent of any crimes against Gaddyl, to sell them as unique slaves to other Fiefdoms!"

Oory said, "Have you supplied him, then, an exact inventory?"

"No, but—"

"I want you to arrange," Oory went on relentlessly, "for that young Normal to escape and one or two Bluies with him. If he seems particularly to fraternize with any, choose them—they will be the ones who know Murno. Use your talents on him, Elder Patron. Cozen him. Remark, casually, that he may soon be seeing some old neighbors of his. Tell him that Murno's family has been captured and is to be taken to Ingress to be interrogated and held as hostages. Now—here is an even more devious part. Let him, and the Bluies he seems to consort with, steal an aircar and escape. Make them think they're very clever about it."

Oj Liave's eyes nictated wildly. "If this is a joke, it is in singularly bad taste. Surely you cannot dream that I—".

Oory said flatly, "I can, and do; and I remind you of vows and old favors you've sworn never to forget. I remind you that a Distorter has been lost and that you and the rest of the Staff are as much to blame as I. And that in doing as I ask, you will be protecting not only Guddun and yourselves—and me, incidentally—but Marshal Stolm as well."

"But . . . but . . . an aircar! Why an aircar?"

"So they can reach Murno quickly, of course."

"But Oory, they would not know how to pilot an aircar!"

"The Gods! Let them capture one of the Volitionless mutant slaves along with it, to teach them. Or use whatever ingenuity is needed. You've done harder things in the past!"

Oj Liave stared at the water as if he'd like to dive into it and escape. After a while he said, "Why Ingress? Simply because you're there now?"

Oory felt his lips draw back involuntarily. "No. A remark was made, and it bit deep. Hear, Oj Liave—Stolm is angry with the Fiefs, and will let them get themselves mired very deep before he calls for help from off-planet. Also, there is the matter of the Distorter on his mind. But he's said that if Wild Folk made a move against Ingress, he'd call for help. And that is what I wish to bring about. Once Colonial Command is brought in, there'll be rules laid down, and an end to this insane slaughter. We'll be able to make peace with the Wild Folk, and—one way or another—I'll have Murno and the Distorter."

Oj Liave twisted his head about miserably. "God of Rain! Do you expect a net of that mesh to draw in fish?"

Oory grinned at him. "Would you care to wager?" While he waited for Oj Liave to find words, he stared eastward, seeing the familiar line of hills but thinking far beyond. After a while he said, "In the last few weeks, Old Friend, I have gained a vast respect for that simple em. Murno will move against Ingress, and his move will be vigorous and cunning. But *I* will be expecting it!"

CHAPTER XXIII: INTERRUPTED JOURNEY

Murno reined in his horse, watching Pel, who (as his eyes were young and keen) rode a hundred yards ahead. The young man had just pulled up at a point where the south edge of the Grove bulged out, and was looking westward. After a moment he reined around and came back at a gallop. "A single aircar, just cruising the edge!"

Murno turned his horse into the Grove. In the last couple of days, he'd learned that the horses wouldn't shy too much if they were walked in slowly so they could get used to the dimness. This was the fifth or sixth time he and Pel had taken refuge in the fringes. "One of these times," he said morosely, "they're going to look closely enough to recognize horses' tracks, and get curious." He reined in and sat for a moment, listening. A bird chirped somewhere. Bird calls and other animal sounds had been noticeable all the way along this southern edge. It hadn't been like this at all when he first entered the Grove from the west—there'd been the hush and the oppressiveness right from the start. Now, clearly, animals from outside were moving into the fringes—yesterday he'd seen cougar tracks, and this morning he'd found the partly-eaten body of a ground-squirrel. And the *feel* of the place was gone. Did that mean a sort of death, caused by the terrible destruction of the northern half? Did it mean that the Grove's master—the Full Blue—was dead? Or merely gone elsewhere? Or withholding his influence from the trees, lest the Gaddyl, or human refugees, learn too much?

Certainly, the change made the Grove far less of a refuge. If, for instance, breloons were put on a trail that led into the Grove, they'd probably follow it now.

He turned his mount westward, pushing through under-growth where necessary, staying just deep enough within

140

the fringes to see. He was anxious to be beyond the Grove and into the dry mountains west of it. How he'd cross the flat land beyond those, and the Sierras if he reached them, were problems for the future. At least, he had Pel—a fair woodsman—with him, and two could travel more safely than one.

He turned to look at the young man; saw that Pel was staring nervously toward the light. "Something bothering you?"

"Well . . . this last aircar I saw was acting differently than the others. It would move a little way, slowly, then pause. And it was staying closer to the trees. The more I think about it . . ."

Murno reined in; looked around for a path. "Maybe we ought to go a little deeper and wait until we're sure it's gone by." He edged his horse a few yards inward. It went carefully, but didn't shy at anything. Pel came alongside and they sat listening.

The horses' hearing proved the better. In a few minutes the two mounts began to cock their ears and turn their heads this way and that. Murno's horse moved its feet nervously.

Then Murno heard it—or felt it; he didn't know which was first. But suddenly his skin prickled; he felt the remembered oppressiveness. And then the trees began murmuring! Very faintly at first, then louder: "Mur-no. Mur-no."

He saw Pel's eyes go wide; saw the young man reach quickly for his bow. Murno restrained a similar impulse. Softly, he said, "Who calls?"

The astonishment on Pel's face was complete when the Grove began to echo—softly—"Who calls? Who-who-who-calls-calls?"

The sound echoed away into silence. Minutes passed. Then suddenly came a voice, a human voice, from outside the Grove: "Murno! It's Liss! Come quickly!"

Murno hesitated only a second. Then he beckoned Pel to follow and nudged his horse toward the call.

At first he thought he was dreaming, or insane. There were Liss and one of his cousins, Kenth's boy Joe, and—most bewildering of all to find sitting in an aircar—Larkan. Finally, he managed to mutter, "How?"

Liss said, "My cousin and I and Joe were captured by Gaddyl. But we stole this aircar and escaped, and came looking for you. We knew where you'd left the Grove going east, and that led us to Larkan's clan—though we had a little excitement introducing ourselves." Liss grinned at the Orse leader. Then he turned serious. "But there's bad news. Bay Fiefdom raided us and captured many. The Old One was wounded. He escaped—but his mind is cut off from us, and we don't know where he is or whether he still lives. And your family . . ." Liss avoided Murno's eyes and gestured at Joe.

Joe said, "The three of us here were hunting when the raid hit. It seemed like the whole sky was full of aircars. We tried to draw them away from camp, but they were dropping gas bombs and we didn't get far. The next thing I knew, we were in the slave barracks west of the bay."

Murno stared dully at the boy. He didn't feel the shock he might have—rather, he just felt let down, beaten; as if a blow he'd expected for a long time had finally fallen. "Was Klayr hurt? Or Sis or Gaje?"

"I . . . didn't see them. From the way Oj Liave talked, they were all right."

Murno tried to remember back. "Oj Liave . . . He used to be a captain of guides . . ."

"He's more than that now," Joe said. "He seemed to be in charge while the Fief was away. He tried to soft-talk me, but I didn't tell him anything. He didn't seem to know I'd crossed the Sack Toe Valley with you."

Murno felt a wild stirring of hope. "Then you don't actually know that Klayr and the kids—"

"He mentioned them. He knew I'd been a neighbor. He said if I wouldn't talk I'd probably be sent from Bay to Ingress, where I'd be interrogated with some of my neighbors. Then sold as a slave somewhere. Maybe even shipped off-planet."

The dull pain inside Murno twinged sharply. He turned away; stared at nothing for a moment; kicked idly at a clump of dirt. At least, he thought desperately, they weren't dead.

Rage finally came. He turned viciously on Liss. "Your people were supposed to take care of them! What was The

Old One doing—out playing games, putting squirrels to sleep or something?"

The blue face quirked in anger. "Many of my people died, Freed Man! I do not know if my own mother and sisters are alive! The Old One may be dead. He fought; that much I know. I—"

Larkan broke in harshly, "When the Gaddyl take a longhorn cow for sport, do they ask how her calves may feel? That's what we are—game animals. That's what we'll stay unless we change things ourselves!"

Murno turned on him, shaking. Then—before hot words poured out—he remembered the man and woman of Larkan's clan he'd come across, slaughtered at their campsite without warning or reason.

A not-quite-sane laugh exploded violently from him. "You wanted to attack Ingress, did you? All right—gather your army! But not all in one place—disperse them in groups, in an arc around Ingress but not too close. Wherever there's good cover and not many Gaddyl. Build up what arsenal you can of Gaddyl weapons. But don't neglect human firearms, or arrows—we're going to need a horde of men, armed however's possible. And horses, There'll have to be some fast maneuvering." He paused to catch his breath. "Don't underestimate the stocks of food we'll need. Meat; cooked or made into pemmican; a lot of it!" He took a stride and faced Liss. "You've got this aircar, and you know how to fly it. I want Kah Let and as many more men of your tribe as you can get here in two weeks. The Old One, if he's able to travel. And the Full Blue—there are things he can do for us, and he may as well help, for there'll be no place for him if we're beaten." He glanced into the Grove. "Can you tell whether there are any Big Ears left here?"

Liss said, "I feel there are."

"Well, you'll have to enlist them—now, if possible; if not, when you come back. Oh—and bring your cats!" He thought swiftly. "Could you control a herd of cattle?"

Liss looked doubtful. "They have weak minds. We could soothe them, or rouse them to stampede."

"In a direction you chose?"

"Yes."

"That's all we'll require."

143

Pel was tugging at Murno's arm. "The word must get to Omha, and to my people!" He turned to Larkan. "Will you be sending messengers east at once? I'd like to ride with them!"

Larkan nodded emphatically.

Murno darted a look at the young Burnie. "Are you insane? You're a fugitive from your people!"

"I'm not a fugitive from Omha! And there are friends who'll stand by me. In any case, my people have a right to know. And who can reach them if I can not?"

Murno hesitated briefly. "All right!" He turned to Larkan. "Listen: we'll allow fourteen days for assembling and equipping, then five more for getting close to Ingress. On the twentieth night, counting tonight, we'll attack. What your messengers can do, besides notifying clans close enough to join in, is arrange a diversion somewhere else early on that night. Do you know where Fiefdom Chunn is?"

"More or less."

"There must be an attack, or a semblance of an attack, there, sufficient to draw part of the Garrison from Ingress. Can you persuade Orse east of the Rockies to handle that?"

Larkan said, "I'll persuade somebody. Do you want it actually overrun?"

"Well . . . not at the cost of a lot of lives."

"Lives," the Orse leader said, "are cheap right now!"

Murno looked at Liss again. "What we'll need from the Full Blue is some sentient plants—small ones, I guess—to do some spying at Ingress."

Liss looked incredulous. "Do you expect him to grow trees in two weeks? And in a place he's never seen?"

"Of course not! We can sneak in a few some way—put the problem up to him! Maybe *you* can make birds carry them in, or something." He considered briefly. "With luck, you and Kah Let and The Old One, if he's able to travel, and the Full Blue, can be back here tomorrow night. Then we'll need several dozen of your men—with the strongest talents—here; or better, a hundred miles southeast, in two weeks. I suppose most of them will have to come on foot. Can they do it?"

144

Liss grinned. "They'll have sore feet. But it can be done."

Larkan made a choking sound. Murno turned to him. "You're going to learn some surprising things about your new allies!"

CHAPTER XXIV: THE NET AND THE FISH

The mountain was one of a pair, about six miles west of the center of Ingress. That put it within good field-glass range of the closest point of the periphery fence, but much farther than Murno liked from the points chosen for attack. Like the other peaks of this range, it was ancient, eroded; with little soil left to cover the crumbling gray rock of its skeleton. But it could and did intercept rain; and, on a little plateau of its eastern flank, there was enough soil to support a few stunted pines. That meager cover was the best he'd been able to find, if he wanted any view at all of the attack. At least, the plateau was high enough to be unattractive to Gaddyl; and its security was no thinner than some he'd relied on in the last twenty days.

If he'd had even an inkling, when he'd set that time-limit, what an enormous job he was undertaking, he'd have had better sense than to try. A year would have been more reasonable.

Now, fighting off sleep, he sat slumped against a pine-trunk and stared dully at Ingress. In the captured aircar (one of seven they now possessed) that had brought them here, The Old One dozed. He said he would recover, but one leg was so badly burned it made Murno shudder. Larkan was on the other side of the aircar, enjoying the ultimate luxury of a nap. The Full Blue was somewhere up the mountain by himself, where he could concentrate. That huge blue man had supplied the only surprise on the plus side in this whole endless nightmare of organizing and scheming and assessing and puzzling and coping that was about to climax—he'd had a few leafy spies in Ingress for centuries!

Not, Murno mused wearily, that they were yielding any worthwhile information so far. That was one more frustration. He'd been stupid, he realized now, to hope for anything like the sophistication of the trees of the Grove.

The afternoon was clear—no chance, this night, of the rain he'd hoped for. With the field-glasses (captured with one of the aircars) he could see most of the major buildings. The Translocation Center loomed huge and cubical above the customs-buildings, travel agencies, shops, and hotels embraced by the southern curve of the Inner Moat. That, of course, was the vital first objective, though there'd be a feint at the north.

Across the inner circle from Translocation was more clear ground than anywhere else in the city—that was Occupation Command, with its barracks, armories, and hangars that must be taken when the vital link of Translocation was cut.

He sighed, pondering the enormity of the attempt, and how little direction he or anyone else was going to be able to provide once it started.

In what part of that green city, he wondered, were Klayr and the children being held? Were they in passable comfort, or shivering in some dank dungeon? Would they be exposed to the fighting?

The Old One said softly, "You allow yourself to brood too much, Freed Man."

Murno turned his head wearily. "How can I help it?" Then he asked once again the old weary question. "Can you sense anything now?"

The Old One shook his head. "I'm sorry. Maybe it's the population of alien minds, or the mechanical and electrical things, or simply that I'm below normal. But I can feel nothing of your family."

"Maybe," Murno said too harshly, "they're already shipped off-planet. You couldn't feel them thirty light-years away, could you? Where are Kah Let and Liss now?"

"In the woods to the south, trying to achieve some order among the Orse as they trickle in. Sander is with them now. I think, Freed Man, that by nightfall there will be no shortage of men. But it will be a ragged force, and Kah Let is disappointed in some way—perhaps there are fewer captured weapons than we'd hoped."

"Sure," Murno said sourly. He lifted the field-glasses— God, how heavy his arms felt!—and turned them toward

146

the wooded hills northeast of Ingress, whence the first feint was to come. Had the hoped-for Orse arrived? They'd be late-comers anyway, not in time to circle and join the main force to the south. And what were the Blues doing about the cattle they were supposed to round up? What if they couldn't get them here in time? And what if they ran afoul of Gaddyl hunting parties?

And somewhere en route was a contingent of Sierra Norms under Bruke, who'd apparently replaced Donnel as Overchief. Their air-rifles and their crude radios might be crucial. Would they be on time?

The Old One said, "Sleep, Murno. You are down to the dregs of your strength. The plan is good, and cannot be changed now. I'll wake you before dark. I feel a little better, and I can stay awake."

"No," Murno muttered automatically. But maybe if he just lay down for a few minutes . . .

Someone seemed to be tugging at him. He came awake bleary and stupid at first. Then he recognized The Old One's touch upon his mind. Somewhere, Larkan was mumbling.

The blue-skinned patriarch said, "There is excitement at Occupation. The diversionary attack on Fiefdom Chunn must have started!"

Murno fumbled for the field-glasses; blinked hard to clear his eyes; got focussed on the distant base. Gaddyl Armsmen were streaming from barracks, buckling on equipment as they ran, and clambering into waiting aircars. The first vehicle rose; hovered. Others joined it. A Flotilla of twelve flashed away northeastward. The second bunch was forming hastily, some of its units still emerging from hangars.

Larkan moved over beside Murno, field-glasses before his eyes. "What's it look like to you? Half the garrison?"

"At least!" Murno told him. The tightness was in his viscera now; his blood was pumping hard, driving away sleep. He watched the troops still emerging from barracks. Most of them gathered into small knots, their hands gesticulating excitedly. They were obviously busy with rumors.

Fiefdom Chunn, a thousand miles farther east, would

already be in darkness. Here, the light was going, so that the field-glasses were of less and less use. But Murno saw more aircars move out of hangars and line up. Squads assembled raggedly but didn't board. Other aircars—unarmored, some of them cargo or transport models—took off nearly empty and flashed away.

The Full Blue suddenly spoke from behind Murno. "I have no trees really close to the Garrison, but there are a few near enough to pick up scraps of talk. The rumors are that Chunn has already been swarmed over by mounted men! Many of the Gaddyl escaped by aircar, or into the big lake there. Personnel and guests are counterattacking from the air, and a bloody fight's developed."

Larkan said tensely, "Good! But I hope the clans have sense enough to grab what weapons they can carry, and get out. By morning they can be safely scattered!"

"By morning?" Murno said dully. "By morning it won't matter, one way or another." He handed the glasses to The Old One. "It's getting too dark for me. Can you tell what's going on?"

The patriarch levelled the glasses; held them steady for a minute, then began moving them about. "More aircars have gone. There are only a few left now. And not many troops are in sight. In other parts of the city, civilians are swarming about. A few private aircars are heading northeast."

Murno said, "Sightseers. That'll add to the confusion, and clutter up the radar screens. What do you feel from our own aircars?"

"Liss is aloft somewhere south, meeting groups of Orse as they arrive and directing them on. At least, that's what I guess from what I feel. Kah Let is aground, arguing with clan leaders. He is exasperated but not deeply worried. To the north, one of my grandsons in an aircar is meeting new arrivals too. I feel . . . yes—he sends an impression of home, and of the snowy peaks—the Sierra Norms have arrived. And there is a sound in his ears; many hoofbeats, I think. And a wariness and a concern regarding the air around him. He's probably afraid Gaddyl will fly near enough to see the Orse he's meeting." He handed the glasses back to Murno. "Lights are coming on, Freed Man; you can see as well as I now."

148

Murno located the garrison again. The grounds seemed almost deserted. Could the attack on Chunn really have drawn away that many Armsmen? There were weapon-positions about the garrison, of course, and they might be manned. He turned the glasses toward the Translocation building. If there was any unusual contingent of troops there, it wasn't in sight.

Would reinforcements already have been asked from off-planet? That had been one of the points he'd had to argue about with Larkan. The Orse leader had been all for making attacks on several widely-scattered Fiefdoms at once. That, Murno said, would be too much—reinforcements would surely be called. The attack on Chunn had to look like an isolated local thing, just serious enough to draw part of the garrison from Ingress. Then, the blow against the capital had to come suddenly, without a hint of warning—and it had to carry through to Translocation in one swift punch.

Thinking over the plan, Murno fretted now as to whether they hadn't leaned too far toward vast numbers. How could they be sure but that even now some part of the army had been discovered? He hadn't, and Larkan hadn't, really comprehended the delicacy of timing they'd need. Would it not have been wiser to settle on a smaller force that could be moved into position in a single night?

That, he told himself glumly, was useless speculation now.

He swept the glasses across Ingress. Gaddyl civilians strolled about the city. There were little knots of gossipers, but no sign of panic. That was good— Command must not have even the slightest worry that there'd be trouble here.

He looked back at Command. "Damn it, it's too deserted. That may mean reinforcements are on the way!"

Larkan said, "Well—if they don't get here pretty soon, it won't matter!"

Murno turned the glasses on the outer circle of cleared land; studied the ring of guard towers. That open space looked dishearteningly wide, and he had some idea of the weapons that would rake it. Lights were on in all the towers—they were manned, whether they all had full complements or not.

The tightness in his stomach was almost unbearable. Would this last few minutes stretch on forever?

The Old One said calmly, "They are beginning to stampede the bovines."

Murno jerked the glasses northward, his hands almost too shaky to hold them. He could see nothing but vague blackness. A point of light moved into the field of view, making him jump—an aircar, he realized; some Gaddyl innocently flying over the wooded hills. It passed out of sight.

He lowered the glasses in frustration.

From two of the towers nearest the north, spotlight beams suddenly lanced out.

He jerked up the glasses. The lights were sweeping along the fence, and beyond it. For a minute he saw nothing—then out of darkness came a surging, kneading mass. The light gleamed off tossing horns. More lights flashed on. Straight toward the fence the stampede came. Suddenly, the radio at Murno's chest began shouting in a shrill tiny voice—some civilian, possibly the one whose aircar-lights he'd seen, was excitedly describing the stampede, via common-band radio. The voice was suddenly cut off by a sound like a pebble being crushed. After that there was silence.

The stampede was nearing the fence now. But these were longhorns, wily and agile enough so that the leaders could swerve, flowing eastward along the fence. Only a few were forced up against the wire—which was electrified only to repel, not to kill. But a pile-up came, and Murno saw one dark bulk crash through the barrier, sprawl, roll to its feet and gallop a few steps before a bullet struck it down. Here and there, now, others broke through. Then a whole section of the fence went down and the herd poured into the cleared circle, turning east along it.

The Old One said, "My relatives have cut through this side of the stampede."

Murno swept the glasses westward along the great curve of the fence. Darkness—but then one of the lights swung that way. A knot of mounted men was galloping toward the nearest tower. Someone—probably in an aircar—shot out the light. There was darkness again for a moment.

But now the fuse was lit—now the sand was running. The call would flash out for reinforcements, and, on some distant world, Armsmen would clamber (if they hadn't already) into fighting ships to be flung here at speeds unimaginable.

Searchlights raked the open ground; the whole ring was ablaze with light now. The first group of horsemen were now spurring their mounts, in a cluster, *away* from one of the towers. Murno didn't comprehend until one of the tower's three legs collapsed—he hadn't seen the ropes. The tower crashed down and the few horsemen still alive spurred toward it. All but two jerked and fell from their saddles as bullets rained upon them, but the two reached the fallen cubicle and leaped into it. He couldn't see what became of them.

The herd was still pouring into the cleared circle an eastward along it. They'd isolate the guards in the towers. Four more towers were in darkness now, probably hit from the air.

So much for the feint! Murno turned his glasses unsteadily to the south.

The distance was farther, but he could tell that as yet the towers there had seen nothing to shoot at. Their lights were sweeping the fence, back and forth. Everything looked peaceful.

The attack there started dramatically.

Two towers went dark; then swiftly, half a dozen more. That would be Kah Let and his nephew in aircars, using the best of the captured weapons. Lights from the other towers raked the sky futilely for a minute, then hastily turned back toward the fence.

Larkan gasped, "Look!"

Into the dim illumination where the towers were knocked out charged an awesome juggernaut—great scaled head swaying from side to side, fearsome mouth agape, mighty limbs flashing in a gallop. Against the jeel's charge the fence was no more than a cobweb. Straight through it hurtled; checked; turned; contorted briefly and bit at its side where a bullet found a vulnerable spot; charged outward and crashed through the fence at a different place. Farther along another scaled monster was already making its jagged entry. Then two more! "God!" Murno breathed, "Four of them . . ."

Now horsemen poured through the gaps. Searchlights raked frantically. A heavy beamer lashed out—but it was obviously in attacking hands, for it sliced through a tower's tripod, letting the cubicle crash down. Murno realized that the faint murmur in his ears was gunfire—almost too distant to hear. He took a step toward the aircar. "We've got to get closer! We can't tell—"

Huge gentle hands took his shoulders. "No, Freed Man," the Full Blue said, "We've got to stay here, safely out of it. We're the nerve-center."

"But how can we expect to—?"

The Old One said, "How could you see anything in the thick of it? We have knowledge: Kah Let is jubilant. Orse have reached the Outer Moat and are spreading around it. Soon, when they have enough men there to give covering fire to swimmers, they'll cross it. In the north, a smaller force has spread along the Outer Moat too. They'll keep some of the defenders busy. Bovines have been driven through the hedge to the Moat, and urged to swim. That will add confusion. And—"

Murno demanded, "Where's Sander?"

The Full Blue said, "He's at the Outer Moat, in the south. I hear his name being spoken."

Murno felt as if he'd burst. "Why don't they push on?"

The Old One sighed. "They must gather into a force. And there has to be *some* scouting ahead of them. Kah Let and Liss are doing that now, in the aircars. I feel their intentness, and their search for hidden danger."

Murno spun to face the Full Blue. "What do you have in the residential zone? And the Inner Moat hedge?"

"Nothing among the residences. Those are carefully-tended gardens and hedges. At the Inner Moat I have a few ears. If the defenders have set up a line, it is not there. Perhaps farther out? A short way inside the Outer Moat?"

Murno snarled, "If Sander would start a few men swimming across, he'd find out! Time's passing!"

The Old One said, "It will not be long. I can feel satisfaction from Kah Let."

"Not long!" Murno echoed bitterly. How could things drag so? Actually, he knew, only minutes had passed since

152

the breaching of the fence. But in minutes, reinforcements could come so very far. . . .

Unable to stand still, he strode out to the very edge of the plateau; swept the glasses back and forth across the area where fighting should be going on. Searchlights from guard towers, isolated but still manned swung futiltly, too far out to provide light. Neither were there any flashes in the dark area. He strained to hear gunfire. There was a faint desultory crackle, an insignificant exchange, which might be from the north.

The pulse in his temples was a hot tide now. Could it be—was it possible to hope—that the way to the big cubical building actually lay clear? Surely, some defense had been mustered somewhere! Maybe it was drawn tight around the Center, confident that mere arrows and rifles could be scorned. Didn't they realize yet that the attackers had a few aircars; a few heavy beamers?

From under the trees The Old One called, "We are starting to swim the Moat. Our aircars are hovering, ready to strike at any resistance. There is a feeling of beasts swimming. . . . Yes, they are taking horses across."

Larkan came running; shouting half-coherently, "They're going to make it!" He pounded Murno on a shoulder. "They'll punch straight through; there's nothing at the Inner Moat either!"

Murno barely heard him; barely felt the pummeling. The glasses shook in his hands. He watched the futile swing of the searchlights, scanned the dark area and saw nothing. An odd feeling began to grow in him, as if this were all unreal. His voice came small and ragged. "They *are* going to make it! That pressure on Occupation, from the north, must have—"

Then—a brief sun bloomed over the dark area. While he blinked, another came, and another. He heard The Old One's stricken cry; turned and ran to the aircar. *"What —?"*

The Old One's eyes were squeezed shut; his face taut with pain or grief. The Full Blue said in a savage voice, "There is noise at the Inner Moat now! Gaddyl are moving in weapons!"

Two more quick suns bloomed and died. And now, suddenly, a ring of searchlights flashed into being above the

Outer Moat—a ring that moved around it, lighting all the wide circle of the Moat, while heavy energy-beams stabbed down! Murno seized The Old One's big shoulder; tried to shake it. *What's happening?* Where are Liss and Kah Let?"

The patriarch shuddered, opened his eyes, drew a ragged breath. "Liss and two of his cousins are dead. Kah Let is badly hurt, and downed in the residential area. *You* have the glasses, Murno. Are you blind? Must I tell you of the lightning that struck?"

Murno, almost too sick to breathe, lifted the glasses; peered through them; lowered them. He took two or three aimless blind steps; half-felt Larkan shaking him; half-heard Larkan's shouted questions. He blinked; seized control of himself. When he spoke his voice was dry and tired. "We were children. There were armed aircars—half a hundred or more—sitting up above somewhere, waiting. They let us start across the Moat—why they waited, I can't guess—then they came down and blasted our aircars out of the sky and started working on the Moat. Look for yourself. They're still using the beamers. Anyone swimming now has the choice of drowning or being boiled alive." Slowly he walked back to the aircar; asked the Full Blue, "What's going on at the Inner Moat now?"

"The defense has been set up, Murno. They're quiet, waiting."

Murno felt already dead inside. He said to The Old One, "I'm sorry I spoke harshly. We have a few men caught between the two moats. Do you have any contact with them?"

The patriarch nodded slowly. "Kah Let has the use of both legs and one arm. He's gathering what men he can, and making his way toard the Inner Moat. But he knows what will wait him there. He expects to die."

Murno said, "We were such fools . . . obviously, they expected us. Well . . . Old One, if you'll climb out of this car, I'd like to use it."

Larkan tugged at him. "Where are you thinking of going?"

"I'm going down and kill as many as I can before they kill me."

The Old One settled himself more firmly in the seat.

154

"Let us not delay, Freed Man. I have this." He displayed a Gaddyl handgun.

Larkan and the Full Blue climbed wordlessly into the back seat.

From a mile away, Murno could see steam rising above the Outer Moat. Beyond, in the clear space, was chaos—bovines, horsemen, riderless horses, and men on foot milled about. A few of the men shot at the aircars. But those cars, of course, would be equipped with Distorters. As well shoot at the moon.

No use, Murno thought mechanically, to get himself and his companions shot down before they could strike even a token blow. And as he couldn't hope to pass under or through the circling ring of aircars, the only way was over. He let the car shoot upward. "They'll see us on radar," he explained absently, "But as long as we're going up, they can't be sure we aren't Gaddyl making a belated evacuation. Then if we come down fast enough, they may not hit us before we land. I'll try to bring us down right over Translocation. We don't have anything powerful enough to do more than scar the building, but . . ."

The Old One said, "Bring us down just within the Inner Moat, Murno! Kah Let will be able to feel where I am. And if we can make any dent on the defense, hitting it from behind—"

"All right," Murno said listlessly. "It doesn't matter. Time's run out anyway." It flashed into his mind that, if he knew where the family was being held, he might No. Insane to hope he might reach them before he was gunned down.

He slowed the descent; got ready to plummet. . . .

On the northern horizon there was a brief glow of light. He stared that way, then shrugged. "Some fighting somewhere else, I guess. Maybe one of our aircars got away." He reached again for the controls.

Larkan seized his shoulder and pulled him forward. Anxiously, he pointed down. "Look!"

A big section of the roof of Translocation had opened. A ship—cylindrical and big as a cottage—rose swiftly from it and darted away laterally. Another followed. "Fighting

155

ships," Murno said, wondering why he didn't feel more concern.

Larkan said excitedly, "Fly into that hole! We can——"

"No. There'll be a Distorter protecting the whole building, of course. We'd be shunted aside to God knows where." He scanned the dark areas just inside the Inner Moat; wondered idly if one of the incoming war vessels might pause to blast him. "Well . . ."

The world seemed to turn to fire. Blinded for a moment, he sat with his eyes shut, clinging to the seat. It was well that he did—for suddenly the car bucked as if it were a fly in the muzzle-blast of a gun. He heard Larkan's startled shout; grabbed for the controls; tried to send the car upward again. It wouldn't rise. Something hit the hull with a sound of tearing metal. They were falling, not fast—the emergency grav had cut in. He peered, still half blindly, over the edge.

Where the big cubical building had been was gaping crater.

Another blast battered at the aircar, and the light—from somewhere behind him—lit Ingress for an instant. The Full Blue said, "One of those ships blew up! It was using beams on a bunch of Orse, out beyond the fence, and——"

Another blast. Then, a minor one—but nearer—and Murno said, "God! That got one of the aircars! We've got to . . ." He cut off the emergency grav and let the craft plummet. He checked the fall when trees rushed up toward them; stared around for the Inner Moat. He chose a dark lawn beside a minor building and maneuvered the car onto it. There were more of the lesser detonations. They seemed to be getting more and more distant, as if the Gaddyl armored aircars were fleeing unsuccessfully. He clambered out of the vehicle. "Into cover!"

The Full Blue helped his limping relative. They pushed into a hedge. Not far ahead, Gaddyl voices babbled in shock and terror. Murno crept forward, gripping a handgun.

A great light bloomed in the sky, but this time there was no blast. Instead, after a moment, a gargantuan voice roared—in English—"OMHA ABIDES!"

Gaddyl were blundering through the hedge now, in an utter rout. One nearly ran into Murno. Murno leaped. He grabbed furiously at the blaster-gun the alien carried, and wrested it away. The alien wriggled free and ran.

The Old One had moved close to the Moat. Now the patriarch lifted his head and called out in a clear tenor voice.

Seconds later he was answered from beyond the Moat.

The last resistance was at the Occupation Garrison, where what remained of the Armsmen plus the gunwise civilians they'd collected were entrenched. There seemed to be no way of getting at them except to blast the buildings to rubble one by one. But after sun-up there was a hail—one of the beseiged aliens was using a loud speaker. He spoke in English. "Hello! We ask a short truce. Is Murno there?"

Murno, startled, climbed to his feet from his sniper's-position. He evaded the hands that reached to restrain him. "They won't break a truce—that's an Armsman talking!" He stepped into sight, knowing the alien's instrument would pick up his voice. "This is Murno."

A minute later a Gaddyl, carrying the portable loudspeaker and a light hunting-rifle, came from concealment and stood looking toward Murno.

Murno stared back. "Oory!"

The alien dipped his head in acknowledgement. "We are a long way from home, Freed Man."

Murno tried not to look at the rifle. "A long way, Your Eminence. What do you want to talk about?"

"Company Prime is the title. I want to tell you something and ask a favor. First: your family is at liberty somewhere in the north of Kalf. We never captured them. That was a deception I arranged to bring you here."

Murno stood dazed. When he tried to speak, his throat was too tight. Finally he managed, "Thank you. And the favor?"

"My own family is somewhere about the world. Now that you seem to be Master, I ask that you show them mercy."

Murno choked down emotion. "They'll get that. Oory—there's no need for you to die! There'll be thousands of your people captive. They'll be put them all in one place—some area with plenty of water and a mild climate. They'll need a leader. You could—"

157

Oory dipped his head. "I'm sorry, but I have another job. I seem to be in command here. Stolm has killed himself." He made a tentative move, then, "Oh. I must ask clemency for my former Fief. But I don't know where he is either."

Murno said softly, "Guddun will be treated impartially, Your Eminence. Kokiel was my Fief too."

"Thank you," Oory said, "And now the truce is ended." He lifted the rifle very deliberately.

The bullet spanged into marble five feet above Murno's head.

The alien turned unhurriedly and walked toward cover. Bullets—arrows—rained around him. Murno saw him hit at least twice, but he did not fall. Somehow he managed with dignity to walk out of sight.

Larkan was suddenly beside Murno. "The sneaking bastard tried to kill you!"

Murno didn't answer for a while. Then, "No. He's a much better shot than that, Larkan." He brooded a little longer. "The use of the rifle was notice he intended to fight to the death. And having me in his sights, and not killing me, was a salute—a recognition of equals, and that my cause was honorable." He turned, weary to the point of collapse. "Bring up some heavy stuff and finish it quickly."

CHAPTER XXV: PAPERWORK

Spring in the new human capital was lovely. Some of the rubble had been cleared; some was already disappearing under new greenery. The Moats and canals ran clear and clean. There were bridges over them now—only a few aircars had power left, and, with no commerce from off-planet, mankind would be dependent on horses for a while.

Murno shoved aside the mountain of paperwork on his desk. What, he wondered, would happen if he simply burned it? Wouldn't people get along somehow? Possibly not, now.

He picked up a microphone and said, "Send the boys in."

Gaje and Joe came in, grinning in their new fabric

clothes. "Well!" Murno said, "Aren't you the dandies! But I suppose the first semester of Omaha Academy has to be launched with a flourish."

"Dad," Gaje said, "Did you know who's going to be human Director there? Pel! Just because he was a priest, or something!"

Murno suppressed a sigh. Already, things were being forgotten. "There's more to it than that. It was the fervency of his plea that persuaded the computer to launch its missiles. If it hadn't been for him, none of us would be here now. I want you to be polite to Pel. And his wife."

Joe said, "I think she's pregnant already!"

Murno sighed. "Well, I wanted to see you before you left, and remind you again to study hard. We have a very short time to learn the technology. Omaha wants to teach us. When the Gaddyl Empire counterattacks—maybe in as little as twelve years—we'll need a real force to fight them off. And you two will be in the forefront."

Gaje said, "All right, Dad." Joe said, "I haven't forgotten, Mr. President, how my family was hunted down."

Murno shook hands with them and let them go.

As they left, one of the two big pale-furred felines wandered in, came to rub briefly against Murno's chair, then patroled around the room sniffing at things. Presently it gave him a look, mouthed a soft complaint, and went out again.

How long, he wondered, would the two cats go on looking for Liss? Maybe he ought to take them out to the western slope of the Sierras, where they'd at least be at home. He could do that when he started the vacation Klayr was demanding he take.

Maybe she was right. Certainly, sitting here at a desk struggling with avalanches of paper wasn't the future he looked forward to. Where he could really be useful, he knew, was in the field. It was going to take a definite effort to keep the various Normals and mutants from splitting up again into their separate societies. The Sierra Norms must be urged to send more of their young men to Omaha. So must the Blues, and the Big Ears. And more of the Orse must be persuaded to visit around—after all, they were the most populous.

And before long he, Murno, ought to visit Kah Let and the Full Blue and The Old One and see what they were up to. Experiments of some sort—and wouldn't they be needed when the Gaddyl came?

And the humans from overseas. Only a trickle so far. And the Burnies. Then there were the newly-freed slaves. He had a couple of those, bright, fairly-well-educated young men, who could read and write English and Gaddyl, for assistants.

Well, all that would have to wait until he got his desk cleared up a little.

He picked up a piece of paper and frowned at it. Someone—an Orse clan he'd never heard of—wanted an extra allotment of steel so they could make their stirrups out of that instead of wood. . .

He sighed and stared at the document unseeingly. Then, suddenly, his eyes focussed on it again. His frown became a scowl.

Carefully, he lifted a pile of documents and slid the one about the stirrups under it. Then he pressed a button to call one of his young assistants.

The young man came in eagerly. "Yes, sir?"

Slowly, Murno got up out of the chair. He took the young man by the arm and gently sat him down. "Try," he said gravely, "not to make the same mistake too often. And do what seems best."

He marched to the door, then paused to look back at the gawking young man. "There are some kinds of slavery," he said, "for which a man has nobody but himself to blame."